Professor When and His T.O.A.S.T.E.R.

The Screenplay

By

Wayne Jarman

Professor When and His T.O.A.S.T.E.R.
The Screenplay

Written and Illustrated by Wayne Jarman

Published by AWL Media
74 Fletcher Street
Edgeworth NSW 2285
Australia

First printed November 2017

Photography by Noel Clarke

Cover Design by Wayne Jarman – based on a photograph by Noel Clarke (Noelyn Studios).
(All rights reserved.)

NATIONAL LIBRARY OF AUSTRALIA

A catalogue record for this book is available from the National Library of Australia

ISBN 978-0-9870931-2-7

Professor When and His T.O.A.S.T.E.R. is a fictional work and the fictional characters depicted are not intended to represent any real persons, living or dead.

Language & Spelling: English (Australia)

Other books by Wayne Jarman:

With a Mind to Achieve
(Personal Development / Success)

To the Honour of the Kings
(Fantasy Fiction)

TO LINDI,
For her positive words, always supporting my mad-cap schemes.
Love you, always.

TO THE RADIO PLAY CAST,
Thank you for your wonderful contribution to this two decade
adventure!
Susan, Trent, Shayne & Gareth.

Connecting with Wayne Jarman:

Email:

awlsystems@gmail.com

Website:

http://www.ReflectiveBubble.com

Stage32:

https://www.stage32.com/WayneJarman

Twitter:

http://Twitter.com/ProfessorWhen

Facebook:

https://www.facebook.com/WayneJarman.Author/

Instagram:

https://www.instagram.com/waynejarman_awlmedia/

THE LOGLINE:

Professor When (an Inventor who is afflicted with 'extrapolated elocution' and a fetish for acronyms and dual-purpose utensils) is visited by two not-so-bright teenagers who trigger events that accidentally send them all back in time ...and history is in serious trouble.

The Radio Play Team:
Shayne Bartlett, Susan McEwen,
Wayne Jarman, Gareth Jarman & Trent Wilson.

Photography by Noel Clarke (Noelyn Studios).

IN THE BEGINNING...

Professor When was written as a Radio Play and recorded in a studio in 1999. At the time, I was 'treading the boards' with a local Theatre Company and had access to some very talented, very professional (in every way other than remuneration) young actors.

As I wrote the script, I visualized Susan Ford (now McEwen) as the young female lead and Trent Wilson (still Wilson) as the young male lead.

Consequently, while still in the creative phase, I was able to use my considerable imagination and name my characters Susan and Trent. (I think the names suit the characters well.)

My son, Gareth, (still at school at the time) showed an interest and I offered him a part – on the condition that he studied, rehearsed and 'measured up'. To his Father's surprise he did ...and conducted his acting role with 'aplomb'.

I roped in our Sound and Recording expert (Shayne Bartlett) for some roles and told him not to be concerned with his lack of acting experience or his lack of rehearsal. I'm not sure what I said all those years ago to convince him to be part of the play, but I do know that in all of his roles he met his Director's requirements perfectly.

Susan dragged along her brother (Michael Ford) and we invited him to be part of the band of Greek Soldiers, who were terrified by Great Zeus' lightning bolt. Lindi Jarman also joined in as part of the fear-filled Greek crowd.

My good friend Noel Clarke (the most wonderful Professional Photographer I have ever met) drove for hours to meet with us and to take Marketing Photos of the cast. With his kind permission, we are able to reproduce his photography within this book. Noel's photos were in Colour but have been converted to Black & White for the purpose of this book. I have also treated them with a 'Film Grain' effect to give them more contrast and a 'film feel'.

The brief rehearsal period and the Recording day constitute my first experience of being a Director. I have had a lot of fun as an actor but the day in the Recording Studio must go down as the funniest day that I have ever spent.

Trying to convert the script to a recorded audio production and bringing the script to life as a comedy while very competent **stage** actors acclimatised to a Studio atmosphere, with the inevitable slip-ups and messing around, had us all literally rolling on the floor.

Shayne's twenty or so attempted recordings of the 'extrapolated elocution' sentence were a highlight of the day and, in the end, we patched it up during the editing process.

We produced ten episodes in that one day which, given the hilarity of the event, was a pretty good result. Mind you, it took another six months for me (with most of the effort and skill supplied by Shayne) to complete the editing process!

Another five episodes were (rather optimistically) written but the Radio Play production has never gained enough commercial interest to warrant going back into the Studio. Though, these further five episodes did come in very handy when it came time to convert the script to a screenplay.

The aim in producing the Radio Play was to create a mad-cap, "thinking man's" comedy. Professor When and His T.O.A.S.T.E.R. could be loosely described as a mix of Monty Python, Doctor Who and The Goons. These were, after-all, the influences on my generation.

Our additional aim in this mixture was to be as accurate (and educational) as possible on the time periods that we entered. The facts of the event are in there but you have to sift through the chaff.

My goal of recreating the Ancient Greek language was, however, overly optimistic. I planned to have the Ancient Greek Soldiers yelling fearfully at Professor When (thinking he was the great God Zeus) in the language of the time. I made contact with Emeritus Professor Godfrey Tanner (now deceased unfortunately) at the University of Newcastle (Australia) to ask for a translation. I expected a five minute phone conversation but spent over half an hour with him. (He was a nice guy.) We corresponded as well but in the end, we had everyone yelling fearful statements at Zeus (Professor When) in English and then, during editing, we ran that segment of recording backwards.

Some sample Episodes of the Professor When Radio Play can be found on the AWLMedia (Official) YouTube Channel and on my website (www.ReflectiveBubble.com).

WHAT CHANGED?

To move from a Radio Play to a Screenplay obviously requires some changes.

The obvious first difference is the formatting style. Screenplays, we are told, have a very definite format and a variety of software applications have been developed to enable the screenwriter to end up with that defined result. Unfortunately, the more time you spend on forums listening to screenwriters, the more you find the advice varies.

I will hold my breath and await the onslaught of advice on what is wrong with the formatting within this book. Fortunately, as an old Engineering Technician, I have a very thick hide ...and I will review the feedback and take what good advice I can.

Another variation is obviously the move from a sound based format (dialogue and sounds to develop images in the minds of the radio audience) to an audio AND visual format. Words had to be included that described what the audience should be seeing. At the same time, the amount of dialogue had to be tempered so that the result wasn't just a radio play on screen. I hope I have achieved that. It wasn't easy to temper the dialogue with a character like Professor When, who does indeed suffer from extrapolated elocution.

Another area that I had to address was the length of the script. Even when I added the five unrecorded episodes of Professor When and His T.O.A.S.T.E.R. to the recorded ten episodes, I still didn't have enough material for a feature length film. As a result, the entire adventure after the toaster leaves the ship (the last fifth of the script) is material created specifically for the screenplay.

Adding this new material, almost twenty years after writing the original radio play material, was a very interesting experience.

When I was writing for the radio play, I saw Susan McEwen and Trent Wilson in their roles and wrote specifically for them and for what I perceived to be their stage acting characteristics. I also wrote Professor When while visualising me playing the role.

Writing the later material as a film script left me with different options. I stopped visualising Professor When with me performing the role and my mind started looking for film actors who fitted the 'style' of the character. I ended up writing (not deliberately) for an older version of Blackadder (Rowan Atkinson). This was partly, I think, because I have always been a Blackadder fan ...but I think I was also affected (positively) by Rowan Atkinson's role as Doctor Who in a Comic Relief parody of the show with Julia Sawalha as his companion. This unintentional change of characterisation took me by surprise.

Another facet of change was the ability to add material that I had thought of after the first ten radio episodes had been 'set in concrete'. For years, I had been imagining how I would start the film and, for some reason, an alien assassin, stalking Professor When, developed in my mind and then became a theme that weaved throughout the script. I now had the opportunity to incorporate this new material. I consider myself fortunate in this respect. This is an opportunity that very few writers are given.

The most noticeable change, however, came from the very fact that I was rewriting almost twenty years later. My attitude to the world had changed. In fact, the attitude of a large segment of the world population had changed. Comedy had changed ...and, on reading some things I had written twenty years ago, I did a bit of a cringe.

There were two subjects that hit me in particular. In the original radio play script, Achilles and Patroclus are overtly gay and Helen of Troy is very fat.

There is nothing wrong with that and there is nothing wrong with incorporating either subject in a comedy setting. In fact, both themes still exist in the screenplay. The changes I made were only subtle ...but they were enough to go from an older comedic effect to a newer style that appreciates some of the human sensitive messages that we send to an audience and that we expand within our communities.

I know! It sounds like I'm just trying to be 'politically correct'. I don't like that term. I think it is an overused sneer at people who have realised the effect that their words and actions have on the well-being of other human beings.

I read an article in which Mel Brooks was commenting that, in today's world, his film 'Blazing Saddles' would probably not have been made. I disagree. I think the film would still have been made ...but the style of the comedy would have reflected modern values, with only nuanced changes.

The point is that what had changed in the twenty years was me and a large part of the world. And that is a good thing. Comedy has changed. That led to subtle changes in the script.

I hope you enjoy reading my screenplay.

"PROFESSOR WHEN AND HIS T.O.A.S.T.E.R."

A screenplay

by

WAYNE JARMAN

INT. A CAR IN A SUBURBAN STREET. DAY

An old, beat-up car is parked at the side of a suburban road. TRENT, a very nervous young man, is at the steering wheel, doing his best to ignore the instructions from SUSAN, an equally young woman who is in the passenger seat.

                    TRENT
          You've only had your licence
          three days. You're not allowed
          to teach me.

                    SUSAN
          Shut up and do what I say.
          You'll have your licence before
          you know it.

Susan is very strong-willed and overbearing. Trent always gives in.

                    TRENT
          So, what do I press to make it
          go fast?

                    SUSAN
          Yes, we'll get to that.

Trent is lost in his imagination.

                    TRENT
          I wanna press the fast buttons and
          shoot fire from the exhaust and go
          sideways and leave wheelie marks,
          just like in the video game.

SUSAN
Yes this will all happen in time,
...by accident.
For now, I just want you to turn
that key to start the engine.

EXT. A LITTLE FURTHER ALONG THE SUBURBAN
STREET. DAY

PROFESSOR WHEN, an elderly gentleman, walks
along the sidewalk. He whistles softly and
is lost in his own world. He carries a
letter and approaches a letterbox.

A GREEN ALIEN slithers along the opposite
sidewalk. It leaves a slime trail as it
struggles to move from garbage to garbage,
seeking cover. It is burdened by a large,
extra-terrestrial rifle.

The green alien stops behind a cluster of
garbages to study the Professor.

The Professor suddenly stops. He realises
that he has walked past the letterbox. He
rotates on the spot, as he seeks the
letterbox and finds it.

                    PROFESSOR WHEN
          Oh!

He smiles at his lapse of concentration. He
looks down at the letter to give it a final
review.

The green alien seizes the opportunity of
the Professor being stationary. It rests its
rifle on the nearest garbage, takes aim and
pulls the trigger. The green light on the
rifle turns red but nothing else happens.

The green alien spits out non-English words that are, nevertheless, obviously swear words. Its voice is high pitched and 'other worldly'.

GREEN ALIEN
Gnarrs non nimper poten!

The green alien studies the rifle, gives it a hit with his soft, slimy hand and tests the trigger again. The light turns green, there is a slight whirring sound and the letterbox vapourises silently.

The green alien studies the result with disgust. He face palms with a wet jelly noise. As he pulls his hand away, strings of slime dangle between his palm and his forehead.

GREEN ALIEN
Gnarrs non nimper poten!

The Professor walks to the letterbox to post his letter. It isn't there anymore. He looks confused and shifts his gaze between the empty space where he thought he'd seen the letterbox and the letter in his hand.

The Professor eventually accepts the situation, puts the letter in his coat pocket and walks back in the direction that he originally came from.

The green alien frantically presses buttons on the rifle. It stares, in disgust, at the red light on the energy pack. The green alien's attention moves between the Professor and the red light.

INT. AN OUT OF CONTROL CAR. DAY

                    SUSAN
          (screaming in panic.)
     The brake pedal!
     The brake pedal!

                    TRENT
          (screaming in panic.)
     I've got it to the floor!

                    SUSAN
          (screaming in panic.)
     The other brake pedal!

EXT. THE SUBURBAN STREET. DAY

The red light on the rifle has finally turned green. The green alien takes aim.

The out-of-control car ploughs into the garbage bins. Bins are everywhere. Trent continues to rev the engine but the car isn't going anywhere.

Professor When walks past on the opposite footpath. He shakes his head at the noise and confusion. He walks on.

INT. THE CRASHED CAR. DAY

Susan is screaming loudly to be heard over
the revving engine.

                  SUSAN
     Take your foot off the pedal!
     Move away from the pedal!

It all goes quiet.

                  SUSAN
        (sarcastically.)
     Thank you!

                  TRENT
     Well, that was fun.
     Now what?

                  SUSAN
     We run away before the cops arrive.
     I will now give you a quick lesson
     on reversing ...and hiding.

EXT. THE LITTERED SIDEWALK. DAY

A close up of the wheels of the car as they
reverse off the curb. A large puddle of
green slime trickles over the curb and into
the gutter. A bin moves and reveals the
green light of the rifle and more trickling
slime. The rifle dematerialises.

The sound of an over-revving engine and the
scream of tyres is heard, fading into the
distance.

INT. INSIDE THE STATIONARY CAR. DAY

Susan is in the driver's seat of the parked
vehicle. She and Trent have ice-cream cones.
They lick them in silence. They are both
bored.

                    TRENT
          We could catch a movie.

                    SUSAN
          Nothing on. Checked.
          Broke, anyway.

                    TRENT
          We could go to the lake.

                    SUSAN
          Oh, God. I'm so bloody bored.

Trent thinks for a while and then his mood
brightens.

                    TRENT
          We could go visit that nutty
          Professor.
          He's always good for a laugh.

                    SUSAN
          Yeah. Let's go.

INT. PROFESSOR WHEN'S KITCHEN. DAY

The Professor works on his toaster on the kitchen table. He uses a bread and butter knife to leverage something on the inside. He wears diamond cutter's glasses and rubber gloves.

Susan and Trent wander in the open door.

                    SUSAN
          Hello, Professor.

Susan is buoyant, in stark contrast to the Professor who removes his glasses and gives her a look that suggests that he still remembers her last visit and he bears some ill feeling.

The Professor releases the knife and takes off his gloves. He responds dryly and with caution in his voice.

                 PROFESSOR WHEN
          Hello young, female type person.

Trent appears from behind Susan and takes an instant interest in what the Professor is doing.

                    TRENT
          Having trouble with your toaster?
          Here, let me help.

The Professor is instantly panicked. He has suffered from Trent's assistance before.

                    PROFESSOR WHEN
        No. Do not touch the eating utensil
        that is currently performing the
        dual purpose of screwdriver and
                    (MORE)

There is an electrical explosion and Trent
vanishes.

                PROFESSOR WHEN (CONT'D)
        ...leverage device. Oh, buggar!

                      SUSAN
        He touched the knife.
        Um, ...where is he, Professor?

                    PROFESSOR WHEN
        He has been transported inside the
        Time Orientation and Searing Toast
        Electrical Receptacle.

                      SUSAN
        He's inside the toaster?

                    PROFESSOR WHEN
        If you care to use the acronym for
        the Time Orientation and Searing Toast

Susan is annoyed with his extrapolated
elocution.

                      SUSAN
        Is he in the toaster? Yes or No!

                    PROFESSOR WHEN
          Confirmation on your enquiry.

Susan slaps him.

                    PROFESSOR WHEN
             Aarh! ...Yes, even.

                       SUSAN
          Just by touching the knife?

                    PROFESSOR WHEN
             Do not touch the
                  (MORE)

The Professor is in mid-sentence when there
is an electrical explosion.

                 PROFESSOR WHEN (CONT'D)
             ...eating utensil that is currently
             performing...
             Oh, buggar!

Two, high, squeaky voices echo from deep
within the toaster.

                 SUSAN(V.O.) / TRENT(V.O.)
             Helllp!

The Professor leans over the toaster and
talks into the bread slot.

                    PROFESSOR WHEN
        You are in no danger. Do not touch
        anything. I will now join you by
        touching this multi-purpose utensil
        and show you how to reverse...
                    (MORE)

The Professor touches the knife and there is
an electrical explosion. His next words are
heard in a high, squeaky voice from within
the toaster.

            PROFESSOR WHEN (CONT'D) (V.O.)
        the miniaturisation and
        transportation process.

INT. INSIDE THE TOASTER. ARTIFICIAL LIGHTING

The three are inside the toaster, ...which is immense! The huge room is filled with electrical machines with flashing lights and regular beeps and whistles that the Professor pays no heed to.

They are standing next to a giant bread and butter knife that is next to a circular control panel. The control panel is covered by dials and meters and buttons and display units.

Trent is exploring the controls and is very impressed.

The Professor puffs his chest out with pride at his invention.

                    PROFESSOR WHEN
          You see, you are in no danger.
          Welcome to the time orientation and

                    TRENT
          Wow! This is great. Everything is
          so large.
          And look at all the electronic gadgets.
          What else can this toaster do?

                    PROFESSOR WHEN
          Well, it is a Time Orientation and
          Searing

                    TRENT
     What does this do?

The Professor panics as Trent's hand hovers
over a red button.

                 PROFESSOR WHEN
     Do not depress the red circular
     button with the inscription that
     says 'Time
               (MORE)

There is an electrical explosion and
clunking mechanical noises. The lights flash
off and on as if something is draining their
power.

              PROFESSOR WHEN (CONT'D)
     ...Travel'.

The scene goes to black but we hear
Professor When's empty voice screaming
through time and space.

              PROFESSOR WHEN (V.O.)
     Oh, buggarrrrrr!

INT. INSIDE THE TOASTER. ARTIFICIAL LIGHTING

It has been a bumpy ride. The lights come back on and Trent and Susan are leaning on the console for support. Susan is annoyed. The Professor is on the floor.

The Professor gets up, dusts himself off and moves to the console.

                    SUSAN
          What happened, Professor?

The Professor reviews the readouts on the console.

                    PROFESSOR WHEN
          Well, according to the external
          audio receptor and visual display,
          we are somewhere in Asia minor
          ...about 3000 years before you
          were born.

Susan slaps him.

                    PROFESSOR WHEN
          Aarh!

Trent laughs hysterically at the Professor's joke.

                    TRENT
          Oh, Professor, you're such a
          fruit cake.

                        SUSAN
        I don't think he's joking.
              (MORE)

Trent stops laughing.

                        SUSAN (CONT'D)
        What do you mean '3000 years' before
        we were born?

                        TRENT
        You're some sort of fruit cake.
        You ought to be locked up!

                        SUSAN
        I don't want to be in Asia Minor!
        I want to be home. Right now!

                        PROFESSOR WHEN
        Ah! Harsh reality dawns on our young,
        involuntary, yet some-what-responsible,
        chronological crusaders.

Stunned Silence.

                        SUSAN / TRENT
        What?

PROFESSOR WHEN
We are all in Asia Minor, 3000 years
before your birth, as a direct result
of you both touching the eating utensil
that was performing the dual purpose
of screwdriver and leverage device in
the Time Orientation and Searing Toast
Electrical Receptacle.

TRENT
What?

SUSAN
We touched the knife in the toaster.

PROFESSOR WHEN
Not forgetting that YOU depressed
the red circular button that says
'Time Travel'.

Trent is momentarily lost in thought as he
recalls pressing the button. A childish
smile crosses his lips. It is not an
intelligent look.

TRENT
Oh, yeah.

SUSAN
I don't care about this.
I want to go home!

                    PROFESSOR WHEN
Unfortunately, the red circular
button that says 'Time Travel' was
depressed before our time was notated
as the origin point within the
electronic circuitry of the
time orientation and

                    SUSAN
You don't know how to get back,
do you?

                    PROFESSOR WHEN
Um, are you going to repeat the
same brutal physical assault which
I encountered when I previously
answered one of your questions?

Susan slaps him.

                    PROFESSOR WHEN
        Aarh!

                    SUSAN
Confirmation on your enquiry.

                    PROFESSOR WHEN
I can get us back. I just need to know
the exact date and time that we now
occupy and I can make the calculations
from there, using now as the origin
point within the electronic circuitry
of the time orientation and

                    TRENT
How do we find that out?

PROFESSOR WHEN
By conversing politely with some
intelligent life form of this period
and ascertaining the time and date,
...of course after reversing the
miniaturisation and transportation
process by which we entered the time
orientation and

SUSAN
Do you think we could call this
a 'Toaster'?

PROFESSOR WHEN
        (with confusion and frustration.)
Yes.
If you must.

TRENT
And you want us to go outside and
talk to someone?

The Professor adopts a very slow method of
speech in the hope of accommodating the
perceived dumbness of his audience.

PROFESSOR WHEN
Yes. ...To ask them the time and date.

TRENT
You are a fruit cake.

SUSAN
OK! Stay cool! Let's go outside
and find out the time and date so
that we can go home.

PROFESSOR WHEN
Good philosophy!
Now everyone hold hands and I will
touch this extremely large eating
utensil which you see before you and

There is an electrical explosion.

EXT. ON A BEACH. DAY

The Professor, Susan and Trent are beside
the toaster. They are on a sandy beach.
There are SOLDIERS, in Ancient Greek
uniforms, looking shocked at their sudden
appearance.

                    TRENT
        It's very nice out here, Professor,
        but who are all these people?

                    SUSAN
        The ones in armour with the shields
        and big swords.

                    PROFESSOR WHEN
        Oh, yes. Pick up the Time
        Orientation and
                (MORE)

Susan slaps him.

                    PROFESSOR WHEN (CONT'D)
        Arrh! ...The toaster!
        And put it under your arm.
        We don't want to be separated from it.
        Be careful not to touch the eating
        utensil

Electrical Explosion!

                    SUSAN
        He touched the knife, Professor.

                    PROFESSOR WHEN
              (talking into the toaster.)
         To reverse the process, simply
         touch the

Electrical Explosion!

                         TRENT
         I'm back.

                    PROFESSOR WHEN
         Somewhere in time and space, someone
         may someday be pleased to hear that.

                         TRENT
         I've got the toaster.

                    PROFESSOR WHEN
         Good boy. Now don't touch anything!

         AGAMEMNON, an impressive looking, older
greek soldier, steps forward.

                       AGAMEMNON
              (speaking in Ancient Greek.)
         EIMAI Agamemnon.

                         TRENT
         What did the big, scary guy say?

                    PROFESSOR WHEN
         I don't recognise the language.
         It's all Greek to me.

                       AGAMEMNON
              (speaking in Ancient Greek.)
         EIMAI Agamemnon.

PROFESSOR WHEN
I think he said 'Agamemnon'.
Oh! This is exciting. Agamemnon was
the commander-in-chief of the Greek
armies attacking the city of Troy.
This is wonderful! We may actually
be in the midst of one of my favourite
periods of history. The Trojan Wars!

TRENT
(sarcastically.)
Wonderful.

SUSAN
Oh, dear.

The situation finally dawns on Trent and he
panics.

TRENT
So, we are in the middle of a war?
What do we do now?

The Professor resumes his slow speech for
dumb people.

                    PROFESSOR WHEN
All we need to do is to converse
politely with Agamemnon to extract
from him the information that we
require on the calendar and
chronological period that we now
inhabit. Then, we simply invoke the
miniaturisation and transportation
process to re-enter the time
orientation and
          (MORE)

Susan slaps him.

                 PROFESSOR WHEN (CONT'D)
Aarh! The toaster, ...and then
re-calibrate the ...toaster...
and return to our origin point.

                    TRENT
          (turning to Susan.)
Translation?

                    SUSAN
We ask the big, scary guy what the
date and time is. Then we go back
into the toaster and go home.

                    TRENT
Oh! Simple!

                    SUSAN
Except that the big, scary guy
doesn't appear to speak English.

              PROFESSOR WHEN
Well, of course not.
Agamemnon is a great, Greek King
and commander-in-chief of a
magnificent, Greek army.
He speaks Ancient Greek.

                    TRENT
So how do we converse politely with
Agamm ...Agamenm ...with Aggy?

              PROFESSOR WHEN
Oh, I simply use my belt.

                    SUSAN
And we use it to thrash him into
submission, until he stops pretending
not to understand English.

There is a pause while the Professor
analyses the level of stupidity.

              PROFESSOR WHEN
    No.
         (MORE)

The Professor produces a gadget that looks
like a T.V. remote control.

          PROFESSOR WHEN (CONT'D)
    This is my belt.

                        TRENT
                (laughing.)
        Professor, you're such a nut case.
        That's not a belt.
        It's a remote control unit.

                    PROFESSOR WHEN
        No. It is a multi-purpose tool
        which has the acronym of B.E.L.T.
        Part of its purpose is as a language
        translator, which accounts for the
        L.T. part of the acronym.

                        TRENT
        Ah!

                    AGAMEMNON
        EIMAI Agamemnon.

The Professor is involved in explaining
technical stuff to Trent and Susan. He
doesn't have time for Agamemnon's
interruption. He Dismisses Agamemnon with a
nod and a wave of his hand.

                    PROFESSOR WHEN
        Yes, yes, yes. In a moment.

Agamemnon looks confused and irritated but
waits patiently. The Professor returns to
his conversation with Trent.

                    PROFESSOR WHEN
        I simply move the indicator to
        'L.T.' and point the belt at this
        great warrior and King ...and
        converse with him.

                    TRENT
What's this switch on the belt do?

                PROFESSOR WHEN
Quiet! I am adjusting the belt so
that I can converse with one of
my greatest heroes.

                    TRENT
But I just want to know what this
switch does?

                PROFESSOR WHEN
Now I point it at Agamemnon and
depress this green button
          (MORE)

                    TRENT
This switch here.

As Trent points to the switch, he
accidentally flicks it to another position.

           PROFESSOR WHEN (CONT'D)
    ...and then I can

The Professor depresses the green button,
mid-sentence. There is a thunderous
explosion. Steaming, little bits of Aggy are
distributed over a twenty metre radius. The
surrounding soldiers respond with excited,
unintelligible Ancient Greek.

                    SUSAN
    Oh! Yuck!

                    TRENT
Ooh! I'm going to be sick.
What did you do to poor old Aggy?

                    SUSAN
You've blown him into a million
grotesque bits.

                PROFESSOR WHEN
             (turning to Trent.)
Did you, by any chance, touch
the switch on the belt?

                    TRENT
Yes, I did.
You were ignoring me!

                PROFESSOR WHEN
Oh, buggar!
B.E.L.T. stands for Blast Emitting
Language Translator. You have
converted the Belt to Blast
Emitter, the B.E. part of the
acronym, and caused me to vapourise
one of the greatest figures in
Greek history
...not to mention, my hero!

                    SUSAN
This is disgusting!
Is the process reversible,
Professor?

                PROFESSOR WHEN
Of course not!

                    SUSAN
OK. Don't get touchy.
It was worth asking the question.

                    TRENT
Professor, I think Aggy's mates are
a bit agitated. Can you understand
what they are saying?

               PROFESSOR WHEN
Of course I can!
I have a Language Translator
        (sarcastically.)
...when the switch hasn't been
fooled with.

                    SUSAN
        (with a level of urgency.)
Use it. They look upset.

               PROFESSOR WHEN
I'll just move the switch to the
L.T. position and point the Belt
in their direction.

The Greek soldiers scream in fear and dive
for the ground. ODYSSEUS, an older, rotund
Greek soldier walks, on his knees, to the
front of the group of soldiers.

                  ODYSSEUS
Please, Great Zeus, forgive us
and spare our meagre lives.

                    SUSAN
That works well, Professor.
I can understand him perfectly.

                    PROFESSOR WHEN
                        (whispering)
          Shh! He thinks I am Zeus, King of
          the Gods.

                      ODYSSEUS
          Please, Great Zeus, stay your
          lightning bolts.

Susan is greatly relieved at the turn of
events.

                       SUSAN
          Well, now that we can communicate
          with these Greeks, Professor

                    PROFESSOR WHEN
                        (whispering)
          Great Zeus!

                       SUSAN
          What?

                    PROFESSOR WHEN
          Call me Great Zeus. They think I
          am the King of their Gods.

Susan and Trent are indignant at the
suggestion and both reply loudly and
emphatically.

                       SUSAN
          I refuse to call you 'Great Zeus'.

                       TRENT
          So do I!

PROFESSOR WHEN
Then they will hack us into tiny,
little pieces with those big swords
that they carry.

SUSAN / TRENT
(loudly and without hesitation.)
Oh Great Zeus, King of the Gods!

PROFESSOR WHEN
Don't overdo it.

SUSAN
(annoyed and sarcastic.)
Please, Great Zeus, ask them the
time and date so that we can go home.

PROFESSOR WHEN
We can't go now.

SUSAN / TRENT
What?

PROFESSOR WHEN
I have just vapourised their
Commander-In-Chief.
I have changed history. We must
remain here until we are sure that
the outcome of the war has not
been changed.

ODYSSEUS
I am Odysseus. Your most humble
warrior.

                    TRENT
     Oh, who cares? Butt out!

Odysseus   meekly   accepts   Trent's   angry
rebuttal.

                   ODYSSEUS
     Sorry!

                PROFESSOR WHEN
     Odysseus! ...or Ulysses.
     A great warrior!

                    TRENT
     No-one cares!
     I want to go home. Now!

                    SUSAN
     Right! Now!

                PROFESSOR WHEN
     I will not go anywhere until I am
     sure that the outcome of this war
     has not been altered.

Trent already understands the hopelessness
of arguing with the Professor.

                    TRENT
     OK! OK! And we can't go home
     until you have reset the circuitry.
     So what is the outcome of the war?

Odysseus   very   politely   and   softly
interjects.

ODYSSEUS
Great Zeus, may I speak?

SUSAN
No, you may not. Shut up!

ODYSSEUS
Sorry.

PROFESSOR WHEN
I will be with you in a moment,
Odysseus.

ODYSSEUS
Thank you, Great Zeus.

SUSAN
Outcome?

The Professor begins counting off the list
on his fingers as if listing the items on
his shopping list.

PROFESSOR WHEN
Yes! The Greeks must win the war.
The city of Troy is sacked and
destroyed.
The Trojan men, women and children
are killed or taken as slaves.

SUSAN
(sarcastically.)
Now there's a goal worth working for.

TRENT
Oh, parts of it could be fun.

PROFESSOR WHEN
But it is very important that the
victory include a large wooden rabbit.

SUSAN
Horse.

PROFESSOR WHEN
No, it's true.

SUSAN
(momentarily confused.)
No. I mean it was a large, wooden
horse.

PROFESSOR WHEN
I'm sure I saw a reference to
a rabbit, somewhere.

SUSAN
Believe me, it was a horse.

PROFESSOR WHEN
I think I am the more educated
on the subject of Troy.

TRENT
I'd go with the Professor.

SUSAN
(turning on Trent.)
Who cares?
It was a horse!

The Professor is unconvinced but wants to
move on.

                    PROFESSOR WHEN
     Well, let's talk detail later.
     Right now, we need to talk to
     Odysseus and sort things out.

The Professor turns his attention to
Odysseus.

                    PROFESSOR WHEN
     Odysseus, how goes the war?

Odysseus smiles broadly at finally being
addressed.

                    ODYSSEUS
     I would be happy to tell you of
     the war, Great Zeus, but would it
     not be better to bring Agamemnon,
     our Commander, back from Mount
     Olympus so that he can answer you?

Susan remains annoyed over the 'horse'
argument.

                    SUSAN
     Yeah, bring him back, Great Zeus.

                    PROFESSOR WHEN
     Quiet slave!

                    SUSAN
What?

                    PROFESSOR WHEN
     I have not sent him to Mount
     Olympus, Odysseus.

                    ODYSSEUS
I thought you had sent him to
Olympus on your lightning bolt.
What have you done with him then?

                     SUSAN
Yeah, what have you done with him?
...Great Zeus.

                     TRENT
Um, this is not a good time for
a domestic. Sharp swords, people!

                PROFESSOR WHEN
               (to Odysseus.)
Um, when did Achilles last fight
in the war?

                    ODYSSEUS
Not for a month, Great Zeus.

                PROFESSOR WHEN
Bring him to me. I will speak
to Achilles about the war and
his attitude.

                    ODYSSEUS
And about Agamemnon?

                PROFESSOR WHEN
Yes, ...if I must.
Now go and bring him to me.

Odysseus and all of the surrounding soldiers
look relieved and immediately run off to
find Achilles, leaving the Professor, Susan
and Trent alone on the beach.

TRENT
They're doing what you tell them to,
Professor.

PROFESSOR WHEN
Of course.
They think I am King of their Gods.

TRENT
We could be very powerful in this
time period, Professor.

SUSAN
Why have you sent for this
Achilles guy, Professor?

PROFESSOR WHEN
Achilles was very important in the
winning of the war.

TRENT
But he hasn't fought for a month.

PROFESSOR WHEN
Exactly! And you will notice that we
and the Greek Armies are standing on
the beach near their ships.

TRENT
So, what's your point?

SUSAN
(slowly and sarcastically.)
That this beach is not inside the
city of Troy.

                    TRENT
              (confused.)
        Is there a beach inside Troy?

                    SUSAN
              (astounded by the stupidity.)
        Oh, no.

                    PROFESSOR WHEN
        Perhaps I can clarify the issue.

                    TRENT
        This could make history.

                    PROFESSOR WHEN
        Due to the varying fortunes of
        battle, the Trojans and Greeks
        often find themselves either on
        the defensive or the offensive.
        When Achilles and his soldiers
        sojourn into battle, then the
        offensive attribute is more
        predominant and the Greeks find
        themselves in the proximity of
        the city. In Achilles absence,
        the defensive attribute is forced
        upon the Greeks and they find
        themselves strategically placed on
        the beach protecting their means of
        returning to their point of origin.
        Now, ...

                    TRENT
        Excuse me, Professor.

Trent turns to Susan with desperation in his
eyes.

                    TRENT
Susan, treat me as dumb as you
like. Use sarcasm if you will, but
please explain to me ...so that
the Professor doesn't have to.

                    SUSAN
Our team's goal line is the city.
The other team's goal line is this
beach. The other team is in our half.
Achilles is a big, burly forward and
we want him to play.

In excitement, Trent hugs Susan and kisses
her on the cheek.

                    SUSAN
Oh, yuck!

                    TRENT
Thank you, Susan.

With a huge smile on his face, Trent returns
to the conversation with the Professor.

                    TRENT
It's alright, Professor.
I understand now.
You don't have to clarify any more.

PROFESSOR WHEN
Oh, that's a very acceptable end
result. I'm pleased that the football
analogy met with your approval and
clarified the 'beach in Troy'
confusion.

TRENT
(to Susan.)
What'd he say?

SUSAN
He said 'that's good'.

TRENT
Oh!

EXT. FURTHER UP THE BEACH. DAY

Odysseus and the soldiers are returning
across the beach, led by two handsome,
muscular young men. One, ACHILLES, has long
blonde hair that flows behind as he runs,
gracefully up the beach. He looks very much
in charge. His good-looking friend,
PATROCLUS, runs beside him, glancing
adoringly at Achilles.

Cut to a close, slow motion shot of Achilles
running. This is a model-type shot to
display his 'beauty' image.

EXT. BEACH. DAY

The Professor, Susan and Trent wait
impatiently on the shoreline.

                    SUSAN
          Professor, why hasn't Achilles fought
          for a month?

                    PROFESSOR WHEN
          Because he argued with Agamemnon.

                    TRENT
               (snickering.)
          Well, he'll never do that again.

The Professor is annoyed by Trent's attitude
toward Agamemnon's demise. He gives him a
dirty look and is about to say something
when Susan intercedes.

                    SUSAN
          He sounds like a bit of a girl.

                    PROFESSOR WHEN
          Well, I wouldn't tell him that
          if I were you.

                    SUSAN
          What was the argument about?

                    PROFESSOR WHEN
          A girl.

                    TRENT
               (still snickering.)
          Well, they'll never do that again.

PROFESSOR WHEN
Young man, I don't believe that
you're treating this situation with
the gravity that it deserves.

TRENT
Sorry, Professor, but wasn't this
war started by an argument over
some tart?

PROFESSOR WHEN
How dare you! 'Tart' indeed!
You are talking about Helen of
Troy. The face that launched a
thousand ships.
How I would like to look upon her.

SUSAN
Professor! You're in love.

PROFESSOR WHEN
Am not! ...And stop calling me
'Professor'.
Here comes Achilles. Call me
'Great Zeus'.

Odysseus and the soldiers return, huddling
behind the protection of Achilles and
Patroclus.

Achilles is loud and aggressive.

ACHILLES
Who dares call the great Achilles
from his rest?

                    TRENT
         (in fear.)
    Oops!

                    SUSAN
         (admiringly.)
    Oh, yum!

                 PROFESSOR WHEN
         (intimidated.)
    Oops! ...Um, it is I, Achilles.
    Great ...aarh ...Zeus.

                  ACHILLES
    Fool of an old man!
    You shall pay for this insult to
    our Gods. Patroclus, my friend!

                  PATROCLUS
         (with a wisp ...er ...lisp.)
    Yeth, my fwend.

                  ACHILLES
    Cut the old fool into sections,
    kill the boy and drag the girl to
    my tent.

                    TRENT
    Oops!

                    SUSAN
    oh, yum!

                  PATROCLUS
    I'm sowy, my fwend, but don't you
    mean 'kiwl the girwl and dwag the
    boy to my tent'?

Achilles, puts his hands on his hips and adopts a very he-man-type pose while looking disdainfully at his friend.

Before any further discussion can take place, Odysseus peeps out from behind Achilles and tentatively puts his hand up to interrupt.

                    ODYSSEUS
     Achilles, before you kill the old man,
     please make him return Agamemnon.

                    ACHILLES
     Why should I care what has happened
     to Agamemnon? He has insulted me.

Odysseus cowers backward a couple of steps.

                    ODYSSEUS
     Well, yes ...but we were planning
     to go into battle later today
     and, well, he is in charge of
     the Armies ...you see ...

Achilles heaves a huge sigh and shakes his head in disgust.

                    ACHILLES
     So where is Agamemnon?

                    ODYSSEUS
     Well, you see ...I believe this God,
     ...um ...old fool, has sent him
     to Olympus.

ACHILLES
Rubbish!
Old fool, where is Agamemnon?

PROFESSOR WHEN
Um, you're standing in him.
Sorry!

ACHILLES
Oh, yuck!

ODYSSEUS
oh, sh ... err!

PATROCLUS
What a wotten meth.

ACHILLES
Oh, yuck!
It's ...he's ...all over my sandals.

TRENT
Yeah! And if you're not nice to us
and the Prof...and Great Zeus, then
you'll be next.

SUSAN
Trent! shhh.

PROFESSOR WHEN
Yes! That's right.
I will take no more of this nonsense.
I am Great King, Zeus of the Gods.
...Um, you know what I mean.

Achilles feels less confident but puts on a
tough act.

                    ACHILLES
I am not convinced.
Prove that you are Zeus.

                    TRENT
Yeah! Show him Great Zeus.
Belt him!

              PROFESSOR WHEN
No! Achilles is a great warrior.
I want him to go into battle
against the Trojans.

                    ACHILLES
I will not return to the war
until Agamemnon apologises.

Silence.

                    SUSAN
Um, I heard him apologise.
Just before he died.

Achilles sceptically narrows his eyes at
Susan and then surveys the myriad of smoking
bits of flesh covering the ground around
him.

                    ACHILLES
Really? Which bit said it?

                    SUSAN
Um. ...You stood on it.

                    TRENT
Aggy is in a million crispy pieces.
How can you still have an argument
with him?

ACHILLES
Very well. If the old man proves
to me that he is Great Zeus, then
I will return to battle.

PROFESSOR WHEN
Oh, yes, I can prove it.
But you won't like it.

ACHILLES
Prove it or die!

PROFESSOR WHEN
Very well.

The Professor points the B.E.L.T. at
Patroclus. Susan panics while Trent folds
his arms, in supreme confidence, and smiles.

PROFESSOR WHEN
Patroclus, could you just step
forward and look toward this please.

SUSAN
(whispering. horrified.)
Professor! You can't belt Patroclus.

Patroclus takes a step forward, in front of
Achilles.

PATROCLUS
Wike thith?

PROFESSOR WHEN
Yes. Just another step to the left,
please.

All of the Greeks are confused by the instruction, and a look of dumb confusion appears on all of their faces. Patroclus, totally confused, just rocks on the spot.

The Professor smiles apologetically as he realises the ambiguity of his instruction.

> PROFESSOR WHEN
> Sorrry! ...Your left, Patroclus.
> (MORE)

Everyone appears relieved by the clarification, except Patroclus who is still thinking hard on the direction. The Professor points in the direction that he wants Patroclus to go.

> PROFESSOR WHEN (CONT'D)
> Your left. Away from Achilles.

Patroclus smiles as he finally understands what is required of him. He takes a long, sideways step away from Achilles.

> PATROCLUS
> Wike thith?

> PROFESSOR WHEN
> Yes. Excellent. Thank you.

Susan is beside herself with worry over what is happening to Patroclus. She whispers a plea to the Professor.

> SUSAN
> Professor!

                    PROFESSOR WHEN
                (whispering.)
Shh! Patroclus died in battle and
Achilles returned to the war to
avenge his death.
Things must get back on track.

                        TRENT
Yeah, belt him one, Professor
...er, Great Zeus.

                        SUSAN
You're both sick.
It's murder.

                        TRENT
Yep.

                    PROFESSOR WHEN
Now, Achilles, you're not going to
like this.
                    (MORE)

                        SUSAN
Neither are you, Patroclus.

                PROFESSOR WHEN (CONT'D)
But I want you to know that I
have to do this because Hector,
the leader of your enemies, has
made offerings to the Gods.
You should avenge your grief
against Hector and his forces.

                        ACHILLES
What should I grieve about?

TRENT
Smile into the gadget, Patroclus.

Patroclus obediently smiles into the gadget.

PATROCLUS
Wike thith?

TRENT
That's it. Good boy!

SUSAN
Oh, you're a sick puppy.

PROFESSOR WHEN
Nothing personal in this, Patroclus,
old lad.

The Professor flicks the switch to B.E. and
depresses the green button. There is a
thunderous explosion. The Greeks respond
with excited, unintelligible Greek that
suddenly turns to English as the Professor
switches back to the L.T. setting on the
B.E.L.T.

ACHILLES
Oh, yuck!
Patroclus, old pal!

ODYSSEUS
oh, sh ... err!
What a mess!

SUSAN
Oh, poor Patroclus.

                    TRENT
    Oh, wow!
    What do you say to that, Achilles?

Achilles and Odysseus share a quick look
between themselves and both go down on one
knee.

               ACHILLES / ODYSSEUS
    Oh Great Zeus, King of the Gods.
    Tell us your commands.

The Professor is rather pleased with himself
that he has got history back on track.

                PROFESSOR WHEN
    Go and fight the Trojans, kill
    Hector, and force them into their
    city. ...And then come back and talk
    to me about a rabbit.

                    SUSAN
    Horse!

               ACHILLES / ODYSSEUS
    What?

Achilles and Odysseus look confused but,
nevertheless, stand to obey the command from
their God. Odysseus starts backing away,
while bowing profusely, but Achilles goes
down onto his knee again.

The panic shows in Odysseus' face and he moves backwards quickly. When he stops, he realises that he is in line with Achilles and Great Zeus. Remembering Patroclus' fate, he takes one huge sideways step to his right.

>   ACHILLES
>   Great Zeus, why have you killed
>   my friend, Patroclus, with your
>   thunderbolt?

Panic shows in the Professor's eyes. He thought everything was resolved and being questioned is not a good turn of events.

>   PROFESSOR WHEN
>   I am sorry, Achilles, but your
>   enemy, Hector, made me do it.

Achilles is not convinced.

>   ACHILLES
>   But how could Hector command the
>   King of the Gods?

>   SUSAN
>   (sarcastically.)
>   Well, there's a good question.

>   TRENT
>   Susan! Shhh!

>   SUSAN
>   (angrily.)
>   Don't shhh me, ...you murderer.

The Professor shows concern. Things are
starting to unravel.

                    PROFESSOR WHEN
          Um, Hector made offerings the,
          ...er, right way. We Gods can't
          refuse when the correct procedures
          are followed.

With this new information, Odysseus has
started to creep closer to hear more.
Achilles is satisfied with the answer and
rises and half turns to go into battle.

                    ACHILLES
          I am so angry!
          I will avenge my friend.

                    PROFESSOR WHEN
                    (relieved.)
          Good boy! Go get him!

As Achilles turns to run, he almost runs
into Odysseus who has crept back into the
conversation. They scare each other.

                    ODYSSEUS
          First, Great Zeus, tell us the
          'right way' so that we, too, can
          command the Gods.

                    SUSAN
                    (still angry.)
          Yeah. Tell him, Great Zeus.

                    PROFESSOR WHEN
                    (whispering.)
You are being less than helpful,
young lady. My aim is to restore
the historical situation so that we
can ascertain the time and date,
reset the circuitry and take you home.
Would you prefer to make this your
new home?

There is silence, while Susan absorbs this
information. She turns on Odysseus.

                        SUSAN
Odysseus, why are you standing there
asking silly questions? Don't you
care that Patroclus has been killed
by Hector?

                        TRENT
You tell him, Susan.

                       ACHILLES
                    (annoyed with Odysseus.)
You never did like my fwend
...um, friend, ...did you?

                       ODYSSEUS
Of course I did.
Patroclus was a sweet guy.

                       ACHILLES
You didn't remember his birthday.

                    PROFESSOR WHEN
                    (impatiently.)
          Gentlemen, the time is ripe to
          avenge Patroclus. Now is the time
          to lead your armies into battle.

                    ODYSSEUS
          I've never known when his birthday
          was. No-one ever told me.

                    ACHILLES
          You only had to ask. But did you
          ask? No! Why should you?
          You didn't like him.

As the argument between Achilles and
Odysseus intensifies, they draw their swords
and pull their shields into a defensive
position. Both look frightened by the
prospect of the fight.

The Professor shakes his head at the
stupidity. He raises his eyes to the sky. He
talks in a sing-song voice because he knows
that no-one will listen.

                    PROFESSOR WHEN
          Hector is your enemy.
          Lead your armies against him
          ...now!

                    ODYSSEUS
          I will not be insulted this way.
          I did not dislike Patroclus.

                    SUSAN
Hey morons!
The one who bashes up the most
Trojans in the next ten minutes
is the one who liked Patroclus
the most.

Achilles and Odysseus both look at Susan and
then at each other and then turn to run up
the sand dune and toward Troy. They are
still arguing as their voices disappear into
the distance

                  ODYSSEUS
It was me.

                  ACHILLES
I loved Patroclus the most.

                  ODYSSEUS
Did not!

Odysseus and Achilles reach the crest of the
sand hill.

EXT. TOP OF SAND HILL ABOVE THE BEACH. DAY

As Odysseus and Achilles reach the crest of
the sand hill, a yellow, slimy, alien life
form lowers itself into the sand so that it
cannot be seen.

The YELLOW ALIEN is surrounded by slimy sand
and has sand stuck to its slimy body. It has
a large, extra-terrestrial rifle. The light
on the energy pack is green.

Odysseus and Achilles run very close to the
alien but they are too busy arguing to
notice it. They puff heavily with their
exertion as they try to talk.

> ACHILLES
> Did so love him the most!

> ODYSSEUS
> Liar, liar. Pants on fire.

The alien waits for them to disappear into
the distance before raising itself onto what
might be elbows to view down onto the beach.
It sees the Professor talking with Susan and
Trent and lifts its rifle, with some
difficulty, into position.

Cut to a long shot of the conversation
between the Professor and Susan and Trent.
The Professor is full of both relief and
self-satisfaction.

PROFESSOR WHEN
Well, we appear to be almost back
on track.

SUSAN
I can't believe that Homer actually
wrote a poem about these dimwits.
The guy must have been blind not to
see how dumb they were.

PROFESSOR WHEN
(astounded by the stupidity.)
Yes. ...Blind.

Cut to a view down a rifle barrel with the
site aimed at Professor When.

Cut to show the yellow alien aiming down the
rifle. It pulls the trigger. The energy pack
falls off the rifle and lands in the sand.

YELLOW ALIEN
Gnarrs non nimper poten!

The yellow alien frantically grabs the
energy pack and tries to wipe off the sand.
It only covers it in slime. It stops as it
hears a noise close by and looks up.

Cut to see a huge Greek soldier, standing
over the yellow alien, with his big sword
raised over his head.

Cut back to the yellow alien. It has a look
of acceptance of its fate. It exclaims
softly in a very alien voice but with
perfect English.

                    YELLOW ALIEN
        Oh, buggar!

Cut to the Greek soldier bringing down his
sword with all his force.

There is a sound like a large mound of jelly
being carved in half.

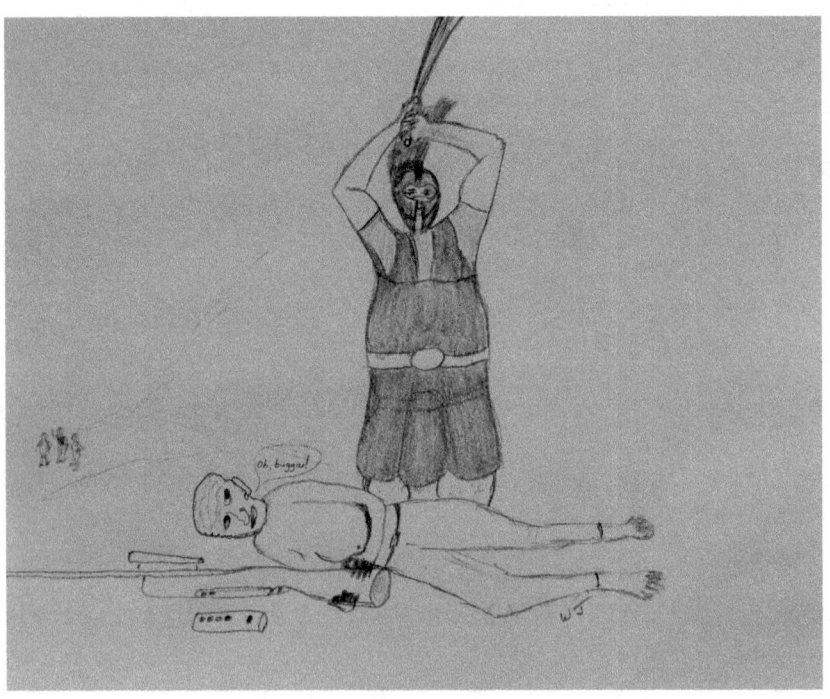

EXT. ON THE BEACH. DAY

There are dim sounds of battle over the sand
hill. At intervals, Greek soldiers run up
the sand dune. The noise and bedlam of
battle increase as the scene progresses.

                    SUSAN
        Can't we go home now, Professor?

The Professor considers the question with a
smug look on his face. He is quite chaffed
with his success. A flash of a Greek uniform
(quite close to the Professor) moves quickly
past.

                    PROFESSOR WHEN
        Yes, well, I do seem to have
        resolved all of the historical
        problems that were detaining us
        within this time period.
        I suppose I could leave a drawing
        of the Trojan...um ...animal.
        Let us instigate the
        miniaturisation and transportation
        process and re-enter the time
        orientation and
                (MORE)

The Professor looks around for the
T.O.A.S.T.E.R. and realises that it is gone.
He screams in panic.

                    PROFESSOR WHEN (CONT'D)
        Aarh! Where is it?

Trent turns to point toward the toaster.

> TRENT
> It's just
> Aarh! It's gone!

> SUSAN
> Aarh!
> You fool! You've lost the Time
> Orientation and Searing Toast
> Electrical Receptacle.

Susan realises that she has said the entire name of the T.O.A.S.T.E.R. and freezes. She calmly stands in complete bewilderment.

> SUSAN
> I can't believe I didn't say
> 'toaster'.

> TRENT
> Someone's stolen our ticket home.
> Call the police!

> PROFESSOR WHEN
> Everybody remain calm!
> Trent has lost the Time Orientation
> and Searing Toast Electrical
> Receptacle.
> (MORE)

He realises what he has said and pauses to be slapped. Nothing happens. He turns to Susan.

PROFESSOR WHEN (CONT'D)
I said it. Why didn't you hit me?

Susan is in a state of shock.

SUSAN
I said it.

Trent reflects and accepts that it is his
fault that the T.O.A.S.T.E.R. is missing

TRENT
I'm sorry, Professor.

The Professor turns to Trent in anger.

PROFESSOR WHEN
Sorry? Why, my dear young man,
there's nothing to be sorry for.
You visit my home uninvited.
You fool with things that you
shouldn't have. You press a button
and take us back 3000 years in time
and then lose our means of returning
home. Why should you feel the need
to apologise?
(MORE)

In his anger, the Professor reaches for the
B.E.L.T. and holds it in front of Trent's
nose.

PROFESSOR WHEN (CONT'D)
Now, would you please look into this
apparatus and smile.

Susan is still lost in her thoughts.

                    SUSAN
      I said it.

The Professor is momentarily distracted by
Susan's utterance.

                 PROFESSOR WHEN
      What?

Trent's very wide, scared eyes look over the
B.E.L.T. that is almost touching his nose.

                    TRENT
      Um ...Susan appears to have gone
      bye-bye, Professor.
           (MORE)

Trent scans around for a means of escape
from the B.E.L.T.
He is suddenly very excited.

                 TRENT (CONT'D)
      There it is!
      The really big guy running up the
      sand hill.

                 PROFESSOR WHEN
      He's running off into battle with
      our property. We have to get it back.
      Come on!

                    TRENT
      Um ...Into battle, Professor?
      You go. I'd better look after Susan.

                    SUSAN
      I can't believe I said it.
      It must be the stress.

                    PROFESSOR WHEN
I'm not going into battle alone.
Either we all go or we all spend
the rest of our days in Asia Minor.

                    TRENT
This isn't such a bad place,
you know.

                    PROFESSOR WHEN
I'm pleased you like your new
environment. We will all spend the
rest of our days here.

                    TRENT
Fine.

                    PROFESSOR WHEN
Together!

                    SUSAN
I can't believe I said it.
          (MORE)

The word 'together' filters through to Susan
and she is instantly snapped back to
reality.

                    SUSAN (CONT'D)
Together?
No! ...I'd rather die in battle.
Follow me.
          (MORE)

Susan yells a battle cry and launches
herself toward the sand hill.

                    SUSAN (CONT'D)
        Let's get our toaster.

Professor When pauses, undecided for a
moment, and then scurries after her.

                    TRENT
        Susan! Come back.

As he climbs the sand hill, the Professor
yells back to Trent.

                 PROFESSOR WHEN
        Come on, lad. Into battle!

                    TRENT
            (confused & frightened.)
        No! I'm not coming.
        Susan! Come back.
        No. Don't leave me here all alone.
        Hold up. I'm coming.
                    (MORE)

Trent runs after them, up the sand hill.
They disappear over the crest while he,
frightened and already puffed, frantically
chases after them.

                 TRENT (CONT'D)
        Stop! ...Please stop.

EXT. TOP OF SAND HILL ABOVE THE BEACH. DAY

As Trent crests the sand hill, he collides with Susan and Professor When, who have stopped to wait for him. They all fall over and scream with the collision.

     SUSAN / TRENT / PROFESSOR WHEN
Aarh!

     TRENT
You didn't have to stop that quick.

They all scramble to their feet.

     SUSAN
Er, yuck! This is almost as
disgusting as the belt.
There are hacked bits and
pieces everywhere.
    (MORE)

Susan shakes her hand and thick, yellow slime trails from her fingers.

     SUSAN (CONT'D)
And where did this slime come from?

     TRENT
I don't like this anymore,
Professor. I want to go home.

     PROFESSOR WHEN
Then let's find our property so
that we can go home.
    (MORE)

The Professor looks around and is suddenly yelling excitedly and pointing.

> PROFESSOR WHEN (CONT'D)
> There it is!

> SUSAN
> Hey you! ...Thief!
> That's ours.

> TRENT
> Tact, Susan.
> Try some tact on the big, scary man with the big sword.

The 'big, scary man with the big sword' is AJAX. He stops and responds with a big, booming voice.

> AJAX
> Who dares call the great Ajax, a thief?

> SUSAN
> Oh! ...You are big, aren't you.
> (MORE)

Susan points at Trent.

> SUSAN (CONT'D)
> He dares call you a thief.

> TRENT
> What?

                    AJAX
      Then prepare to die, little man.

                   TRENT
      Um, Professor, what do you know
      about this 'great Ajax'?

The Professor is lost in his admiration of
Ajax and in his delight at actually meeting
this great warrior.

                PROFESSOR WHEN
      Oh, a great warrior. Second only
      to Odysseus and Achilles.

                   TRENT
      Um, is he supposed to die in
      the war?

The Professor laughs at Trent's lack of
knowledge on the subject of the Trojan wars.

                PROFESSOR WHEN
      Oh, no. Of course not.
      Ajax lived through the war.
      A great warrior.

                   TRENT
           (disappointed.)
      I don't suppose you could belt
      him anyway?

                PROFESSOR WHEN
      Of course not! That would be
      changing history.

>   AJAX
>   Come, little man.
>   Prepare to die.

Trent replies to Ajax in a friendly and
amicable voice, in the hope of placating the
huge warrior, while he negotiates with the
Professor.

>   TRENT
>   In a moment, Ajax.
>   Please be patient.
>   (MORE)

Turning back to his discussion with the
Professor.

>   TRENT (CONT'D)
>   He returned home then?

>   PROFESSOR WHEN
>   Oh, no. He died by his own sword
>   after the war because Agamemnon
>   said that Odysseus was the better
>   warrior.

>   TRENT
>   Who said?

>   PROFESSOR WHEN
>   Aga ...Oh, I see!
>   (MORE)

The Professor giggles at his near oversight
and produces the B.E.L.T. from his pocket.

PROFESSOR WHEN (CONT'D)
Whoops! Almost left a loose end.
Ajax, would you please look at this
apparatus and smile.

AJAX
Like this?

SUSAN
Yes. That's wonderful. ...Thank you.

PROFESSOR WHEN
Nothing personal, my friend.

The green button is depressed with the now
familiar explosion and distribution of
smoking, fleshy bits. Trent is both excited
and relieved.

TRENT
I'll get the toaster, Professor.

Trent runs, tentatively (tip-toeing through
the 'mine field' of flesh so that his shoes
don't get messy), over to the toaster,
retrieves it from the ground and returns to
Susan and the Professor.

SUSAN
Now can we go home?

PROFESSOR WHEN
Well, now that we have regained
the time orientation and searing
toast electrical receptacle

Susan slaps him.

                    PROFESSOR WHEN
Aarh!

                        SUSAN
It's alright. ...I've recovered.

                    PROFESSOR WHEN
Oh joy. Oh rapture.
Now, let's go home.

There has been a growing sound of people
running toward them. Odysseus and several
Greek soldiers arrive. They all go down on
one knee before the Professor, who looks
particularly unimpressed to see them.

Odysseus and his soldiers babble in Ancient
Greek until the Professor produces the
B.E.L.T. and changes the setting back to
L.T. The Greeks recoil in wide-eyed fear.

                      ODYSSEUS
Oh, mighty Zeus. I come to beg
your assistance.

                    PROFESSOR WHEN
Sorry. Must go! Can't possibly stay
another moment.

                        SUSAN
By the way, what day and year
is it?

                      ODYSSEUS
What?

PROFESSOR WHEN
Forget it, Odysseus.
It doesn't matter.

SUSAN
(in anger.)
What do you mean 'it doesn't
matter'? The only reason we came
out of the toaster was to find out
what time we were in.

PROFESSOR WHEN
Ah, yes. As a matter of fact, it
has since dawned on me that the
Greeks used a different calendar
which I don't have a conversion for.

Odysseus has his hand in the air. He wants
to talk but he is pointedly ignored. He and
his soldiers change the knee that they are
kneeling on. Odysseus puts his hand back up
and waits with a bored expression on his
face.

SUSAN
So, even if he told us his date
and time, it wouldn't help?
We needn't have come out of
the toaster.

PROFESSOR WHEN
Well, you do seem to have grasped
the essence of the matter.

A confused Trent turns to Susan, looking for
a translation.

> TRENT
> What'd he say?

> SUSAN
> He said he's an idiot and he's
> risked all our lives for no reason.

Odysseus gives up waiting and interrupts.

> ODYSSEUS
> Mighty Zeus, we have done as
> you commanded.
> We have driven the Trojans to the
> gates of their city and Achilles
> is locked in single combat with
> Hector. We need your assistance
> to ensure that Achilles will win.

The Professor really wants to leave and he
can feel the pressure of Susan and Trent's
gaze. They all need to leave.

> PROFESSOR WHEN
> I'm sure that Achilles can look
> after himself.

> TRENT
> Hear, hear! Let's go, great Zeus.

> SUSAN
> Yep! Let's go!

ODYSSEUS
If you refuse to help, our warriors
may lose heart and the Trojans
will win.

PROFESSOR WHEN
Oh, buggar!

TRENT
I want to go home!

SUSAN
Yeah! Let's go home, great Zeus!

PROFESSOR WHEN
Oh, buggar!

Trent and Susan look at each other and shake
their heads as they acknowledge that they
will not be leaving soon.

TRENT
Oh, alright. Let's go give Achilles
some moral support and then let's
go home. Hate this place!

SUSAN
Oh, alright.
But make it quick, Great Zeus!

PROFESSOR WHEN
I'm really getting tired of
being called that.

EXT. OUTSIDE THE WALLS OF THE CITY OF TROY.
DAY

Achilles runs around the walls of Troy with
HECTOR in pursuit. Both warriors, weighed
down by their armour, shield and sword, are
puffing, sweating profusely and labouring
under their exertion.

The Greek soldiers surround the race and
look particularly bored with events. A scan
of the Trojan soldiers and general Trojan
populous on the walls of Troy, shows that
they are equally bored.

                    ODYSSEUS
          There they are! Hector is chasing
          Achilles around the city walls.

                    SUSAN
          Why is Achilles running away?

                    TRENT
          Dumb question, Susan.
          Look at the size of Hector.

                    PROFESSOR WHEN
          This isn't how it's supposed to be.
          I'm really starting to doubt the
          validity of Homer's account.

                    SUSAN
          I told you before, the guy must
          have been blind.

                    PROFESSOR WHEN
              (astounded by the stupidity.)
         Yes, ...blind.

                    TRENT
         Is Hector supposed to die,
         Professor?

                    PROFESSOR WHEN
         Call me Great Zeus!
         Achilles is supposed to kill him
         in mortal combat.

                    SUSAN
         Well, that's obviously not going to
         happen anytime soon!

                    TRENT
         Not unless Hector has a heart attack
         while chasing Achilles around Troy.

                    PROFESSOR WHEN
         Oh, buggar!

Odysseus anxiously looks around at his
soldiers.

                    ODYSSEUS
         Our mighty warriors are losing
         heart, Great Zeus.

                    SUSAN
         Do you not hear how stupid that
         sounds?

Odysseus is offended by Susan's comment and
does his best to ignore the slave girl.

                    ODYSSEUS
Great Zeus?

                 PROFESSOR WHEN
It shouldn't be up to me! Achilles
is a great warrior. Surely he has
a battle strategy!

Odysseus is confused by the words but is
excited by the prospect of a plan.

                    ODYSSEUS
He may have, Great Zeus. What
does this 'battle straight E.G.'
look like?

There is silence while the Professor, eyes
wide, digests the meaning behind the
question. There is no concept of a 'battle
strategy' in this Ancient, Greek Army.

Face palm from both Trent and Susan.

                     SUSAN
             (sarcasm.)
Oh, you know. Just like your
average unbent, fighting example.

They all look, with exasperation, at Susan.

                     TRENT
Not helpful, Susan.

                     SUSAN
Well?

ODYSSEUS
Have I said something wrong,
Great Zeus?

PROFESSOR WHEN
No, you have answered my question
perfectly, Odysseus.

Odysseus beams with satisfaction at having
done so well.

Achilles' scream can be heard as he
approaches, completing another lap, with
Hector in pursuit, close behind. He looks,
pleafully, at Great Zeus as he lumbers past.

ACHILLES
Arrrrh!

TRENT
It's not going to get any better
than this, Prof ...Great Zeus.
I think it is up to you.

PROFESSOR WHEN
Oh, buggar!

SUSAN
Come on, Great Zeus. We want to
go home.

Achilles does a u-turn and dodges Hector's
sword swing. They run back toward the
Professor. The Professor takes aim with the
B.E.L.T.

PROFESSOR WHEN
I'm really tired of the bloodshed.

TRENT
Me too!

SUSAN
At last!

The Professor flicks the switch to B.E. and depresses the green button. There is a thunderous explosion. The Greek warriors respond with excited cheers. The Professor returns the switch to the L.T. setting.

Odysseus yells in triumph.

ODYSSEUS
Hector has been destroyed by
Great Zeus' thunderbolt.

SUSAN
Oh, yuck!

Amid all of the excitement, Odysseus becomes even more agitated and jumps up and down on the spot, while he points toward Troy.

ODYSSEUS
Look! Helen stands on the walls of
Troy to see Achilles' great victory.

The Professor becomes equally excited.

PROFESSOR WHEN
Helen! I must get closer.
I must see her face.

The Professor and Odysseus begin running toward the walls. Susan and Trent are aghast at yet another diversion.

> TRENT
> Professor! Stop!

> SUSAN
> Come back, Great Zeus!

> TRENT
> Oh, buggar! ...After him!

Susan and Trent run after the Professor. They scream at him to stop, as they run, but he pays no attention. Eventually they all stop within sight of the people on the wall.

The very excited Professor shows no sign of his exertion in running the distance but Odysseus, Susan and Trent are all very red faced and puffing to the point of having difficulty talking.

> PROFESSOR WHEN
> Look! On the wall. Is one of
> those women really Helen of Troy?

Achilles runs past on his victory lap, arms raised high in boastful exuberance, to the cheers and adoration of his warriors. He chants the one line over and over.

> ACHILLES
> I am the champion.
> I am the champion.

                    ODYSSEUS
Oh, shut up, Achilles.
Yes, Great Zeus. She stands next
to King Priam, beside the banner.

Achilles voice fades as he continues his
victory circuit.

                    ACHILLES
I am the champion.

                PROFESSOR WHEN
Helen of Troy! How exciting!

                    TRENT
Who cares?
I want to go home.

                    SUSAN
Yeah! Home!

                PROFESSOR WHEN
What, ...next to the little fat one?

Odysseus is bewildered by the Professor's
inability to understand his simple
direction.

                    ODYSSEUS
Um, ...she stands next to King Priam,
beside the banner.

                PROFESSOR WHEN
            (dejected.)
She is the little fat one
...isn't she?

Odysseus is still bewildered. He narrows his
eyes and talks slowly to the Professor, as
if he is not very intelligent.

                    ODYSSEUS
        She stands next to King Priam,
        beside the banner.

The Professor is annoyed with his tone and
with the situation. He narrows his eyes and
replies to Odysseus slowly, as if he is not
very intelligent.

                  PROFESSOR WHEN
        This is the face that launched a
        thousand ships.
        I think you're all very silly.

                    TRENT
        She's got six chins, at least.
        You're all mad!

                    SUSAN
        Well, I don't think it matters that
        she's cuddly.
        Would it have made this war any more
        sensible if she had been skinny?

Silence, as each of the men look at each
other, realising that there is no safe
answer. Eventually, Trent opens his mouth to
speak and the Professor has a moment of
panic.

                    TRENT
        I'm not dumb enough to get involved
        in this conversation.

The Professor's eyes widen with surprise as he realises that there is a ray of hope for Trent.

                    PROFESSOR WHEN
        Trent! ...My boy!
        I do believe that we may be able to
        save you after all.

Trent is only confused by the attempted compliment.

                         TRENT
        What?

                    PROFESSOR WHEN
        Oh, well. I suppose tastes and
        fashion change over time.
        Even in women.

                         SUSAN
            (sarcasm.)
        Never mind, Professor.
        You still have me.

                    PROFESSOR WHEN
            (far from impressed.)
        Yes, ...quite!

The familiar chant, faintly announces yet another lap by Achilles. The Professor gets back to the business of returning home and turns to give instructions to Odysseus.

                    PROFESSOR WHEN
        Odysseus, ...

                    ACHILLES
        I am the champion.

They have all had enough and, in unison,
yell back at Achilles.

   ODYSSEUS / PROFESSOR WHEN / SUSAN / TRENT
        Shut up, Achilles!

Achilles only looks back in bewilderment at
his hecklers, as he continues his run. He is
only slightly deflated but soon gets back
into being adored by his warriors.

                    ACHILLES
        I am the champion.

They watch him until he cannot be heard
above the cheers of the warriors. Odysseus,
sensing an important moment, returns to the
conversation with the Professor.

                    ODYSSEUS
        Yes, Great Zeus?

                 PROFESSOR WHEN
        Take this note and follow the
        instructions carefully. It will
        tell you how to finish the war.

                    ODYSSEUS
             (excited.)
        Oh, thank you, Great Zeus.

PROFESSOR WHEN
Trent! Put the ...toaster ...down
and everyone join hands and Trent
can touch the eating utensil that

There is an electrical explosion!

Susan McEwen (Susan), Trent Wilson (Trent),
Wayne Jarman (Professor When).

Photography by Noel Clarke (Noelyn Studios).

INT. INSIDE THE TOASTER. ARTIFICIAL LIGHTING

                    PROFESSOR WHEN
          I do wish that you would allow me
          to finalise my sentence to the point
          of the full stop before

                    SUSAN
          You still don't know the time and
          date. How are you going to take
          us home?

                    PROFESSOR WHEN
          I can approximate and guesstimate to
          within a century or two and talk to
          some intelligent life form and

                    SUSAN
          So we are not going straight home?

                    PROFESSOR WHEN
          You have drawn that conclusion
          without awaiting the full stop
          that would have indicated that I
          had reached the end of my senten
                    (MORE)

Susan slaps him.

               PROFESSOR WHEN (CONT'D)
          Arh!
          No. We are not going straight home.

                    TRENT
          Can I reset the circuitry,
          Professor?

The Professor has become increasingly annoyed by this conversation and he is now totally indignant that Trent would even ask to reset the circuitry of his beloved T.O.A.S.T.E.R.

PROFESSOR WHEN
No, of course you may not.

He quickly presses a button and deftly twists a knob.

PROFESSOR WHEN
There! I've done it.

TRENT
That was it?

There is an electrical explosion and clunking, mechanical noises. The lights flash off and on as the power is diverted to the engines.

This experience is different to their last and the Professor looks up at the lights, with concern. The lights do not go off completely and his brow knots with worry as they return to full power. The noises stop.

TRENT
We seem to have stopped.

There is a huge explosion and a glare of blinding white light from within the T.O.A.S.T.E.R. console.

                    SUSAN
What was that?

                PROFESSOR WHEN
Oh, dear. That's not good.
One of the capacitors appears to
have self destructed within the

Both Susan and Trent look horrified at the
prospect of being stuck in time with a
broken part of the circuitry.

                    SUSAN
Do you have a spare?

The Professor is supremely confident in his
answer and somewhat amused by their concern.

                PROFESSOR WHEN
Of course I do.
It's sitting on my kitchen table
at home. I was just about to change
it when you arrived.

                    TRENT
Professor! If its sitting on your
kitchen table at home, then you
don't have a spare!

                PROFESSOR WHEN
Oh, yes I do. You see, it's a matter
of location rather than existence.

Susan is close to a melt down and this
conversation is not helping.

                    SUSAN
I'm sure I would normally enjoy
this philosophical discussion,
Gentlemen, but my mind is
preoccupied with stress and panic.
Do we know how to fix the problem,
Professor?

The Professor takes a second to formulate
his answer.

                  PROFESSOR WHEN
Well. ...There

                    SUSAN
        (yelling.)
Use 'yes' or 'no' and nothing else
...or die!

The Professor's contemplation turns to fear.
He answers meekly and without conviction.

                  PROFESSOR WHEN
Yes.

                    SUSAN
Good boy!
Do you need anything from outside?
...Yes or no?

                  PROFESSOR WHEN
Um ...yes. I need

                    SUSAN
Good!
Let's go outside.

Susan and Trent grab each of the Professor's arms and Susan touches the immense knife. There is an electrical explosion.

During a break from the Radio Play:
Wayne Jarman (Professor When / Patroclus / Ajax),
Gareth Jarman (Achilles),
Susan McEwen (Susan),
Trent Wilson (Trent),
Shayne Bartlett (Agamemnon / Odysseus / Narrator).

Photography by Noel Clarke (Noelyn Studios).

EXT. THE DECK OF A LARGE SHIP. EVENING

It is extremely cold and the water is very
rough. There are deck chairs but no-one else
is in sight. Trent puts the toaster under
his arm and states the obvious.

                    TRENT
        It's a ship, Professor.
        We're at sea.

                 PROFESSOR WHEN
        Oh, good. When we get to shore,
        I'll get the part I need and

                    TRENT
            (in panic.)
        Ah, Professor.
        The life preserver says 'Titanic'!

          PROFESSOR WHEN / SUSAN / TRENT
        Oh, buggar!

Susan resumes her melt down.

                    SUSAN
        You madman!
        Of all the places to drop us!
        I don't want to drown on the Titanic.

The Professor immediately sees the error in
her statement and begins, good-humouredly,
correcting it.

PROFESSOR WHEN
My dear young lady.
You cannot drown 'on the Titanic'.
You can drown in the Titanic when
it is full of water or you can drown
in the ocean, ...but

SUSAN / TRENT
Shut up, Professor!

TRENT
You're babbling, Professor.
Get us off this boat.

PROFESSOR WHEN
'Ship', my boy.
A boat is much smaller.

SUSAN
Oh, God!

The Professor is lost in his nautical line
of thought.

PROFESSOR WHEN
Or a submarine.
A submarine is a 'boat'.

TRENT
We're in the hands of an idiot.

PROFESSOR WHEN
But I don't know whether submarines
were all that common in 1912.

                    SUSAN
     Oh, Professor.
     Come back to us.
               (MORE)

The Professor looks Susan in the eyes,
thoughtfully, and gives every indication
that he has returned to the problem at hand.

               SUSAN (CONT'D)
     Professor. Titanic!

There is a profound silence while the
Professor eyes Susan intently. She waits
patiently to hear his escape plan.

               PROFESSOR WHEN
     Remind me to research the history
     of submarines. Particularly around
     the decades

                    TRENT
          (yelling.)
     Professor!

               PROFESSOR WHEN
     Um, yes?

                    TRENT
     Get us out of here, Great Zeus,
     before we all drown.

                    SUSAN
     Oh, this is awful.

               PROFESSOR WHEN
     Oh, no! This is going exactly to plan.

SUSAN
I don't think he lives on the
same planet as the rest of us.

TRENT
He's not even orbiting the right star!

SUSAN
We are about to run into an iceberg
and drown. How are things 'going
exactly to plan'?

TRENT
(to himself.)
Since when did we have a 'plan'?

PROFESSOR WHEN
We know, within a month, where in
time we are. It is 1912 ...March
or April ...and we can easily
converse with some English speaking,
intelligent life form to find out
the date and even Greenwich Mean
Time. That's a vast improvement
over being somewhere around 1000BC,
surrounded by buffoons who speak
Ancient Greek.

                    SUSAN
          (sarcasm.)
You're absolutely correct,
Professor. I apologise for not
seeing it earlier. It is so much
more comforting to die of drowning
in a close neighbour to our own
century than die by the sword in BC.

                    TRENT
          (sarcasm.)
Yep! I feel much more relaxed now.

               SUSAN / TRENT
          (yelling.)
Get us out of here!

They have been preoccupied with their
conversation and haven't noticed an elderly,
well-to-do couple, MR POSH and MRS POSH,
walking toward them.

Cut to Mr and Mrs Posh.

                    MR POSH
Oh I say! Do keep it down, chaps.

Everyone is shocked at the sudden appearance
of the strangers but the Professor recovers
quickly.

Cut back to the Professor.

                PROFESSOR WHEN
Very sorry. The children are
over-excited.

                    SUSAN / TRENT
What?

                    PROFESSOR WHEN
Shh!

The couple nod and continue to walk past,
noses in the air. Their voices are only just
audible to hear their subsequent comments.

                    MRS POSH
Alfred, I do believe that one of
those 'chaps' may have been a girl.

Mr Posh casts a glance over his shoulder.

                    MR POSH
Surely not, Elizabeth.

Mrs Posh casts a glance over her shoulder.

                    MRS POSH
No. On second thought, Alfred,
I do believe that you were correct.

                    SUSAN
What?

                    PROFESSOR WHEN
Shh!

                    SUSAN
I'm gunna mop the floor with the
toffs. Let me at em.

Susan begins to move in the direction of Mr and Mrs Posh.

                    TRENT
          Go get em, Susan.

The Professor stops her in her tracks with some quick thinking logic.

                PROFESSOR WHEN
          We are stow-aways. We don't want to
          attract any attention to ourselves.
          Do you want to end up in the brig
          of a sinking ship?

Susan immediately stops and returns to Trent and the Professor.

Trent has been thinking. Clearly, not one of his best cards.

                    TRENT
          Professor, the ship doesn't have
          to sink. We could save everybody.
          We could talk to the captain and

                PROFESSOR WHEN
              (shocked at the suggestion.)
          My dear boy! You almost changed the
          outcome of the Trojan wars and now
          you want to save the Titanic and the
          lives of all those on board.
          You really are a chronological
          criminal.

                    SUSAN
        Trent's right!
        We could prevent a catastrophe.

                    PROFESSOR WHEN
        How ridiculous!
        Certainly not!
        It wouldn't be right.

Susan and Trent are both silent as they
study the Professor. The difference between
them is that Susan is thinking. She sidles
up to the Professor and plants a thought.

                    SUSAN
        If we don't get the toaster fixed,
        it would probably be a good idea to
        save the Titanic.

                    TRENT
        I'm with Susan. If the toaster can't
        be saved, let's save the SS Titanic.

                    PROFESSOR WHEN
        R.M.S.

                    SUSAN / TRENT
        What?

                    PROFESSOR WHEN
        Ah! An interesting snippet for the
        nautically inclined amongst us.

                    SUSAN
        Not interested.

                    TRENT
Me either.

              PROFESSOR WHEN
'SS' stands for Steam Ship whereas
the Titanic was, in fact, RMS Titanic.

                    SUSAN
Still not interested.

                    TRENT
Still don't care.

              PROFESSOR WHEN
'RMS' stands for 'Royal Mail Ship'
which means it was contracted to the
British Government to deliver mail.
It had a whole deck ...'G' deck,
I believe, ...allocated to just mail.

                    SUSAN
Not even listening.

                    TRENT
Wait. Are you saying that this is
not a Steam Ship?

Susan stares aghast at Trent, amazed that he
has been suckered into the Professor's
waffle.

The Professor chuckles good humouredly at
Trent's naive question.

              PROFESSOR WHEN
Oh, my dear boy! Yes, of course it
was still a Steam Ship but the

Susan snaps and screams at both of them.

> SUSAN
> Enough!
> Sinking ship!
> Broken toaster!
> Drowning Susan and Trent
> ...and drowning mad Professor.
> (MORE)

The Professor and Trent are immediately silenced. If they had planned to respond, it was overridden by Susan's plan.

> SUSAN (CONT'D)
> I vote that we talk to the captain and warn him about icebergs. Then we can fix the toaster when we reach shore.

> TRENT
> I'm with Susan.
> You're outvoted, Professor.

The Professor stands tall and adopts his best 'captain' voice.

> PROFESSOR WHEN
> As my default chronological crew of the Time Orientation And Searing Toast Electrical Receptacle, do you understand the consequences of mutiny at sea?

> TRENT
> No! And what's more, we don't care.

                    SUSAN
        I'm with Trent.

                    TRENT
        That's right. We're a team.
        All for one and one for all.

                    SUSAN
        Yeah. That's us.

The Professor continues to stand tall and
captain-like while he considers his options.

                PROFESSOR WHEN
        You have no understanding of the
        consequences of mutiny at sea,
        do you?

                    SUSAN
        None.

                    TRENT
        Nope!

The Professor tries his best to sound
official.

                PROFESSOR WHEN
        It involves a firing squad.

The Professor gives every indication that he
is unsure of the firing squad bit.

                    SUSAN
        Do you have a firing squad?

TRENT
Can't see a firing squad.

PROFESSOR WHEN
Maybe it's hanging?

Both Susan and Trent fold their arms across
their chest and move closer, threateningly
close, to the Professor.

SUSAN
You and what army?

TRENT
Yep.

The Professor can see that the position he
has chosen is, in fact, quite weak.

PROFESSOR WHEN
This level of ignorance is difficult
to counter even with historical and
nautical knowledge.

SUSAN
Yep!

TRENT
Ignorance is my super power.

Trent's statement was meant to impress and
intimidate but he has crossed the line. They
both glare at his self-professed stupidity.
The Professor tries a different tack.

PROFESSOR WHEN
Well. What if I say I can easily
fix the toaster and take us
straight home?

TRENT
I'm with you, Professor.

SUSAN
What?

TRENT
How soon can we go, Professor?

SUSAN
Judas! What happened to the team?
All for one and one for all?

TRENT
What do you need to fix the
toaster, Professor?

PROFESSOR WHEN
Well, I need a simple capacitor
and a special ingredient to fill
it with.

SUSAN
          (sulking.)
Morons!

TRENT
I like fiddling with electrical
gadgets, Professor?

                    SUSAN
Really?

                    TRENT
I'm sure I can scrounge a capacitor
out of some gadget on this boat.

                    SUSAN
Ship!

                PROFESSOR WHEN
Good boy! While you do that, I'll
ponder on a particular solution to
providing this special ingredient
that hasn't yet been discovered.

                SUSAN / TRENT
What?

Trent immediately transforms from a state of
excitement to disappointment and anger.
Susan is delighted that her cynicism has
proven to be well-founded.

                    TRENT
Professor, you had me all excited.
I thought for a brief moment that
you might actually be sane.
Susan and I are going to talk to the
captain. Aren't we, Susan?

                    SUSAN
Who are you calling 'we', Judas?

                    TRENT
     Oh, Susan?

Cut to a beautiful young woman, MISS POSH,
dressed in the finest apparel of the day, as
she turns a corner and walks toward them. As
she approaches, the Professor addresses her.

                 PROFESSOR WHEN
     Excuse me, Miss.
     Could you please tell me the time.
     My fob watch appears to have stopped.

She casts the Professor a beautiful smile
and then speaks in a very cultured, friendly
voice.

                  MISS POSH
     Oh you poor man.
     There's nothing more exasperating
     than a stopped watch.

Susan is annoyed at the interruption to her
angry outburst. The Professor relishes this
early twentieth century moment.

                 PROFESSOR WHEN
     Quite!

Trent is in love. He wants to say something
to impress the young lady.

                    TRENT
     Yeah. The battery must be flat.

                  MISS POSH
     I do beg your pardon?

The Professor panics at Trent's anachronism.

>   PROFESSOR WHEN
>   Oh nothing! He babbles.
>   (aside to Trent.)
>   Shut up, my boy.

Trent is confused. He doesn't know what he
has done wrong but the young lady gives him
a compassionate look ...so he is OK with the
flow of the conversation.

>   MISS POSH
>   Oh, I see. Poor lad.

Trent smiles at the young lady's kind words
but she doesn't notice as she is looking at
her watch.

>   MISS POSH
>   The time is 11:30pm.

>   PROFESSOR WHEN
>   Why thank you so much. May I
>   also trouble you for the date?

Miss Posh giggles at the question and
blushes a little.

>   MISS POSH
>   Oh, I see.
>   You and your companions have
>   really spent too long in the bar,
>   haven't you?

                    PROFESSOR WHEN
          Um. Yes. I am rather embarrassed
          to say that we have somewhat
          overdone things.

Susan rolls her eyes at the rubbish
conversation that is going on in front of
her. Trent looks at Miss Posh with big,
puppy eyes and searches for the words to
impress her.

                         TRENT
          Yeah. Um. Quite right.

Susan is close to throwing up. She looks at
Trent with disdain.

                        SUSAN
          Yeah. You bet.

                      MISS POSH
          Sir, it is the last hour of the
          fourteenth of April.

Miss Posh gives a little curtsy and beams a
brilliant smile before moving on.

                      MISS POSH
          Good night.

                    PROFESSOR WHEN
          I thank you for your kindness,
          young lady.
          Good night.

                    TRENT
     Oh, Professor. She's so lovely.
     And did you hear her voice?

Susan is less than impressed with the delay
and keen to get back to the business of not
drowning on the Titanic.

                    SUSAN
     Yeah, gorgeous.
     How many days have we got before
     the iceberg, Professor?

               PROFESSOR WHEN
     Ten minutes.

               SUSAN / TRENT
     What?

                    SUSAN
     The Titanic is going to hit the
     iceberg in ten minutes?
     Get us out of here! Now!

                    TRENT
     Yeah. I don't want to get wet.
     I already had a bath this week.

The Professor is captivated by Trent's
statement. He lifts an instructional finger
as if to begin a lesson. This creates panic
within Susan.

                    PROFESSOR WHEN
What 'week', my boy?
Think about it!

                       SUSAN
Oh please don't get distracted.
I'll be standing on ice talking
to a penguin before we get back
on track.

                       TRENT
Oh yeah.
That bath was in the future.
I'm actually ahead of schedule.

The Professor chuckles at the paradox and
sees an opportunity to display his sense of
humour.

                    PROFESSOR WHEN
Well, that's one way of looking
at it. Or you could say that you
haven't had a bath since 1000 BC.

The Professor and Trent share a laugh at
their own humour. Susan seethes.

                       SUSAN
Stop this, please!
Please get back on track.
Iceberg, gentlemen.
Ten minutes, gentlemen.

Both Trent and the Professor are
disappointed to have their moment spoiled.
They are about to respond to the killjoy but
notice Mr and Mrs Posh walking toward them.

Cut to Mr and Mrs Posh.

                    MR POSH
          (complaining to Mrs Posh.)
     These people really are quite
     intolerable, my dear.

                    MRS POSH
     Even on a maiden voyage of a ship
     like this, you still have to suffer
     the riff-raff.

Susan is in no mood to pretend to be nice.

Cut to Susan.

                    SUSAN
     Up your nose, morons.

Mr and Mrs Posh don't look back but increase
their walking speed. Mrs Posh can be heard
to make a final comment as they move out of
hearing range.

                    MRS POSH
     No, I don't think it can be a girl.

                    SUSAN
     Ooh, I hate them.
     They're so bloody posh.

PROFESSOR WHEN
Yes. That is probably a correct
usage of the acronym.

SUSAN / TRENT
What?

The Professor is delighted to have an
opportunity to enlighten his young, fellow-
travellers.

PROFESSOR WHEN
Well, you see, 'posh' is an acronym
for 'port out, starboard home'.
The only way for the wealthy to travel.
Good grammatical usage, Susan.
I'm very impressed!

Susan doesn't care about the compliment on
her grammar.

SUSAN
Oh, God. I can feel my last minutes
slipping away.

Trent catches on to Susan's desperation and
tries to bring the conversation back 'on
track'.

TRENT
What's this plan that you mentioned,
Professor?

PROFESSOR WHEN
Plan?

There is a short, uncomfortable delay while the Professor gives them both a blank stare. Suddenly, his eyes widen as he remembers their plight.

                    PROFESSOR WHEN
          Oh, yes. Plan!

                    SUSAN
          There is no plan, Trent.
          There has never been a plan.

                    PROFESSOR WHEN
          Oh I beg to differ, young lady.
          Now if you will both excuse me for
          a minute.

                    SUSAN
          One of the few that we have remaining.

                    PROFESSOR WHEN
          I will go into the time orient
          ...the toaster and get what I need.

The Professor reaches across to the toaster in Trent's arms and touches the knife. There is an electrical explosion and he is transported inside the toaster.

Trent and Susan lean over the toaster and hear the Professor singing in a thin, echoed voice. They both react despondently.

                    PROFESSOR WHEN
     Then man the capstan off we go as
     the fiddler swings us round. with a
     yo heave ho
     ...Aha! Here it is.
                         (MORE)

There is another electrical explosion and
the Professor reappears, startling both
Trent and Susan.

               PROFESSOR WHEN (CONT'D)
     Now that I have my capsule, I can

                         SUSAN
                    (dryly.)
     It's a toy gun with a suction cup.

                    PROFESSOR WHEN
     Young lady, you have learnt very
     little in the last 3000 years.
     This is my capsule. Capsule is
     an acronym for Compressed Air
     Propelled Suction Utensil
     - Length Extending.

It's a gadget so Trent is very interested.

                         TRENT
     Does it have a dual purpose,
     Professor?

The Professor is delighted that Trent has
shown an interest in one of his inventions.

                    PROFESSOR WHEN
Of course it does, my boy.
You see this purple button here.

                         SUSAN
Five minutes to a very cold swim.
Is the capsule part of the plan?

                    PROFESSOR WHEN
Yes. Of course it is. I will
explain as we walk to the front
of the boat.

                         SUSAN
          (sarcasm.)
The bow of the ship.

                    PROFESSOR WHEN
Yes. The sharp, pointy bit.
No time for pedantic semantics,
young lady. Time is of the essence.

Susan rolls her eyes in exasperation.

                    PROFESSOR WHEN
Trent, I will entrust you to carry
the capsule.

                         TRENT
Oh, thank you, Professor.

The Professor hands the capsule to Trent who
has difficulty juggling it with the toaster.

EXT. AN UPPER DECK OF THE TITANIC. EVENING

Looking through the sights of a rifle. The
crosshairs are on Professor When, on a lower
deck, as he talks excitedly to Susan and
Trent.

Pull out to reveal an orange, slimy alien
aiming a large, extra-terrestrial rifle and
adjusting its position to get a better shot.
The ORANGE ALIEN glows in the darkness and
is lying in a pool of glowing orange slime.

A red light on the rifle turns green. The
alien's face contorts into what might be a
smile. It settles itself and poises, ready
to pull the trigger.

Cut to the crosshair shot of Professor When,
who suddenly moves toward the front of the
ship, with Susan and Trent, and out of the
crosshairs.

Pull out to reveal the orange alien peering
over its rifle scope as it searches for its
target. The Professor is no longer in view
from the alien's vantage point.

                    ORANGE ALIEN
          Gnarrs non nimper poten!

As the alien begins to move to a different
location, the power pack falls off the very
large rifle and the green light turns red.
The alien rolls his bulbous eyes in
frustration and repeats its curse loudly.

ORANGE ALIEN
Gnarrs non nimper poten!

With great difficulty, and an even greater
amount of slime, the alien repositions the
power pack. It grimaces as it sees that the
light stays red and shakes its head.

The alien slithers off to gain another
vantage point. It finds its movement to be
very easy and fluid on the ship's metal deck
and moves relatively quickly, dragging
behind its lethal weapon.

The rolling motion of the ship on the rough
seas causes it to cut a waving, slimy path
as it slides from one edge of the deck to
the other.

EXT. A DECK OF THE TITANIC. EVENING

The Professor is moving at speed, followed
closely by Susan and Trent. They are headed
to the pointy end of the boat.

> PROFESSOR WHEN
> We should be able to see the
> iceberg when we reach the front.
> Hopefully it will be blue.

> TRENT
> Why 'blue', Professor?

> PROFESSOR WHEN
> Because the blue ones are more
> compacted and contain the
> micro-organisms that I need.

Susan is hearing a flaw in the plan and is
becoming sceptical.

> SUSAN
> What if it isn't blue, Professor?

> PROFESSOR WHEN
> Then we will have to resort to
> plan B.

Susan is suspicious. They are still trying
to work out what plan A is.

> SUSAN
> Do you have a plan B, Professor?

The Professor is exasperated with her need
for detail.

                    PROFESSOR WHEN
          Well of course not.
          We don't need a plan B yet.
          Let's not waste our time on plan B
          when the iceberg might be blue
          ...as per plan A.

                    SUSAN
          Doesn't plan A involve a capacitor,
          Professor?

The   Professor   is   becoming   thoroughly
exasperated now and starting to puff from
the exertion of walking all the way to the
front of the boat. He opens his mouth to
reply but is interrupted by Trent.

                    TRENT
          I've got a capacitor, Professor.

Trent opens his hand to show the capacitor.

The Professor is delighted with Trent's
effort and rounds on Susan.

                    PROFESSOR WHEN
          See. Isn't it good that at least
          one of the team is being proactive
          instead of searching for problems?
                    (MORE)

The Professor turns to Trent and pats him on
the shoulder.

PROFESSOR WHEN (CONT'D)
Good boy. That's exactly what we
need. Where did you get that from?

Trent glows at being praised. Susan turns
dark.

SUSAN
Can we discuss the cute little
detail bits later. It doesn't
matter where it came from. Let's
get on with this plan, whatever
it is.

PROFESSOR WHEN
Look! There's the iceberg!
And we're in luck. It's blue.

SUSAN
(sarcasm.)
Oh buggar!
What a terrible waste of plan B.

PROFESSOR WHEN
Now the plan is coming to fruition.
You see, young people, the advantage
of planning is

SUSAN
(confused.)
That can't be the right one,
Professor. We're going to miss
that iceberg. It's no danger to
the Titanic.

The Professor and Susan and Trent all strain
to see the iceberg in the darkness and study
its position relative to the direction of
the Titanic.

                PROFESSOR WHEN
      Well, perhaps you are right
      ...but it is blue and we need a
      chip off it.

                TRENT
      So how do we get some of the iceberg,
      Professor?

                SUSAN
          (still confused.)
      I don't see any other iceberg.

                PROFESSOR WHEN
      Hand me the capsule, my boy, and I
      will show you.

Cut to a couple walking toward the pointy
end of the boat. The Professor, Susan and
Trent try to act casual as the couple pass.
(They don't do a very good job of acting.)

The couple are GENERAL POSH (an older,
military-style of man) and LADY POSH, an
attractive young woman wearing the finest
clothing and jewellery.

                LADY POSH
      Oh, General, your war stories are
      always so interesting.

                    GENERAL POSH
     Why thank you, my dear lady.
     So, you see, in this instance,
     the Boers were taken completely by
     surprise. Our little ruse worked
     just like a Trojan rabbit.

The General laughs at his own story and Lady
Posh politely joins in. The Professor is
getting anxious. He is watching them walk
slowly across the ship and the iceberg
racing quickly alongside.

                    LADY POSH
        Oh, General, you're so clever.

The couple turn to walk back, out of sight,
on the other side of the ship. The Professor
swings into urgent action but Susan only
shakes her head disappointedly at the
Professor.

                    SUSAN
     Trojan rabbit!
     Oh, Professor.

                    PROFESSOR WHEN
     See! I told you it was a rabbit.
     Trent, hand me the capsule.

                    TRENT
     Professor. There's something I
     should tell you about the capsule.

                    PROFESSOR WHEN
              (laughing good-humouredly.)
          Oh, my boy, there is nothing you
          can tell me about the capsule.
          I designed and built it myself.

                    TRENT
          But...

                    PROFESSOR WHEN
          Quiet please. I am concentrating.

                    SUSAN
          Something tells me that you
          should listen to Trent, Professor.

                    PROFESSOR WHEN
          Quiet, both of you.
          One minute you are hurrying me
          because we only have a few minutes
          and now you are preventing me
          from concentrating on my target.
          Please be quiet while I take
          aim with the capsule.

The Professor takes aim. There is an
explosion as the capsule fires. The suction
cup flies through the air and hits its
target. The Professor is very proud of his
marksmanship.

                    PROFESSOR WHEN
          There! Perfect shot!
          The suction cup is attached to
          the iceberg.

Trent is very relieved that the capsule has worked so well.

>   TRENT
>   Well, that worked ok.

The Professor is quite chuffed that his plan is going so well. He is feeling very confident.

>   PROFESSOR WHEN
>   Of course it did. How could you
>   possibly doubt that it would.

>   SUSAN
>   What now, Professor?

>   PROFESSOR WHEN
>   Now I tie the steel rope around
>   this sticky out piece of metal
>   bit here.

>   SUSAN
>   You haven't spent much time around
>   boats, have you, Professor?

>   PROFESSOR WHEN
>   Oh, I'm sure I would have at some
>   stage. Long time ago, though.
>   Now I turn on the little motor in
>   the capsule and pull the iceberg
>   toward us.

The Professor presses the green button and the electric motor can be heard, pulling the iceberg toward the Titanic.

Again, Trent is relieved that the capsule is working so well.

                    TRENT
        That works ok, too.

Susan is concerned about this plan.

                    SUSAN
        It's coming toward us, Professor.
        Or we're going toward it?
        It's moving very fast.
        Is this safe, Professor?

                PROFESSOR WHEN
        Oh, yes. I only want it to come
        close enough for us to get some of
        the ice and then I will touch the
        reverse button and the steel line
        will stiffen and push the iceberg
        away again.

                    SUSAN
            (in great concern.)
        I think it's close enough,
        Professor.

                PROFESSOR WHEN
        Yes. We can reach that. Now I
        simply press the red, stop button.

The Professor presses the button but the
electric motor continues to whirr.

                    PROFESSOR WHEN
         Um, now I simply press the red,
         stop button a second time.

He presses the button again. Still nothing.
He presses the button, in wide-eyed panic,
again and again.

                    PROFESSOR WHEN
         Just give me a moment, while I
         construct plan B so that we can...

The Professor's voice trails off as he
diverts all of his brain effort to thinking
of a Plan B.

EXT. AN UPPER DECK OF THE TITANIC. EVENING

A very weary orange, slimy alien is aiming
its large, extra-terrestrial rifle at
Professor When. It has wiggled underneath
the guard rail to get a clear shot.

The red light on the rifle turns green.
Again, the alien's face contorts into what
might be a smile of self-satisfaction. It
settles its soft, orange, slimy finger on
the trigger.

EXT. THE POINTY END OF THE TITANIC. EVENING

The Professor has stood still for a while, pondering the nearing collision with the iceberg. A plan B would be good about now but nothing has come to mind. At the point of 'no return' he yells his command to Susan and Trent.

PROFESSOR WHEN
Stand back, everybody.

The Professor, Susan and Trent turn and run.

The ship and the iceberg collide. The noise is intense as the iceberg tears open the side of the ship and buckles the deck where the Professor, Susan and Trent had been standing.

EXT. AN UPPER DECK OF THE TITANIC. EVENING

The orange alien is thrown, by the
collision, into a slimy slide that sends it
against the inner wall of the deck. The
rifle falls out of its hands as it shows
signs of pain.

It reaches for the rifle but is in full
slide as it bounces and slimes its way back
toward the seaward side of the deck.

                    ORANGE ALIEN
          Gnarrs non nimper poten!

It travels under the guard rail and falls a
large distance to the sloping cover of a
motor housing. It groans as it bounces and
slides off the cover to fall another painful
distance.

It lands with a wet jelly noise on the deck
and groans another soft, pitiful curse.

                    ORANGE ALIEN
          Ohhh ...Gnarrs non nimper poten.

The alien seems to have come to rest when a
second shock rolls the ship yet again.

                    ORANGE ALIEN
          Oh, buggar!

The alien free-slides under the guard rail and off the ship. It splashes into the water. A few bubbles reach the surface and then a large area of water turns orange as the alien dissolves like a marshmallow in hot coffee.

Would you travel through Time & Space with this man?
(Wayne Jarman as Professor When.)

Photography by Noel Clarke (Noelyn Studios).

EXT. THE POINTY END OF THE TITANIC. EVENING

Sirens are sounding, PEOPLE are screaming and running.

Cut to a montage to show the chaos.

Cut back to Trent, standing quietly, surveying the damage.

                    TRENT
     Um, that didn't work so well.

The Professor surveys the resulting damage and chaos. He stares, accusingly, at Trent.

               PROFESSOR WHEN
     So ...I am left with the bewildering
     questions of 'where did the capacitor
     come from' and 'why didn't the red
     stop button work'.

                    TRENT
     Um, Professor ...

               PROFESSOR WHEN
     Shut up!
     Pick up a piece of blue ice and
     place it in the capacitor and let's
     go back to the ...toaster.

Susan stares, wide eyed, at the Professor.

                    SUSAN
     Professor, you sank the Titanic.

                    PROFESSOR WHEN
Did not!
It was going to sink anyway.

                        SUSAN
It was going to miss the iceberg.

                    PROFESSOR WHEN
Probably because our weight on
this side of the ship had affected
the steering mechanism. If we
hadn't been here, it would have
run into the iceberg.

                        SUSAN
Sure!

                        TRENT
Professor ...What have you done?

                    PROFESSOR WHEN
I have had enough of this. Let's
repair the time orientation and
searing toast electrical receptacle.
Bring the capacitor, Trent.

They walk, hurriedly, down the ship, looking
for a surface where they can repair the
toaster. People are running everywhere in
panic. Chaos reigns.

                        TRENT
Professor, we've got to help all
of these people.

                    PROFESSOR WHEN
     Hand me the toaster and the
     capacitor.

Trent is suddenly very excited.

                         TRENT
     Look! Here comes that lovely,
     young lady.

                    PROFESSOR WHEN
     Please hand me the toaster and
     the capacitor.

Trent is lost to love. He waves and screams
to the young lady so that she will hear him
above all the hysteria.

                         TRENT
     Young lady!

She doesn't hear him, so he moves to stand
in her way.

Her eyes pierce through him as she speaks
coldly and deliberately.

                       MISS POSH
     Sir, this ship is sinking and
     you're standing between me and
     the lifeboat.

Trent castes her a friendly, confident
smile. He is going to save her and then she
will be in love with him, too.

                    TRENT
     Don't worry. I'm a time traveller.
     I'll look after you.

Miss Posh replies with a voice from hell
...or the gutters of London.

                  MISS POSH
     Move aside or lose it, Bozo!

Miss Posh charges at Trent and sends him
flying to the deck with her shoulder.

                    TRENT
     Aah!

The Professor and Susan rush to assist him
before he is trampled. As they approach him,
he is yelling at the surrounding throng of
people.

                    TRENT
     I've been hit by a front-row
     forward. Who was that gorilla?

                   SUSAN
     That was your lovely, well-spoken,
     young lady.

The Professor is becoming exasperated with
the continued interruptions to his toaster
repairs and decides to try some psychology.

                PROFESSOR WHEN
     Come on, Trent. Get to your feet.
     We have to help all of these people.

Trent struggles to his feet with the
assistance of Susan, ...a disgruntled look
on his face.

                    TRENT
          Me! ...Help them?
          This is how it's supposed to be,
          Professor.
          Can't change history, you know.

                    PROFESSOR WHEN
          We should go home then?
          Is that what you are saying?

                    TRENT
          Yep. I want to go home.

                    SUSAN
          Yep. Let's go.

                    PROFESSOR WHEN
          Excellent. We are finally on track.

Susan and Trent look around at the chaos of
the sinking ship with wide eyes.

                    SUSAN
          How is this on track?
          We are on the deck of a sinking
          Titanic with a broken toaster.

                    TRENT
          How is this on track?

The Professor puts the toaster on a level
surface, smiles and lifts an instructional
finger.

SUSAN

Don't do it! There will be pain.
Just get on with the repair.

PROFESSOR WHEN

No! It is only right that I should
explain why our problems are over.

SUSAN

Make it quick.
Use acronyms, where applicable.

TRENT

Yep. Summary version!

PROFESSOR WHEN

We are back on track because we have
not changed history in either Asia
Minor or the North Atlantic.

SUSAN

Horse!

TRENT

Let the rabbit go, Susan.
Please talk faster, Professor.

PROFESSOR WHEN

We are back on track because we
know the exact time and date and we
can precisely set our instruments
to take us home to the precise time
and date that we want to arrive home.

SUSAN

I'm glad we chose the summary version.

                    TRENT
     Let him finish, Susan.

               PROFESSOR WHEN
     We are back on track because we have
     a capacitor filled with the correct
     ingredient to repair our time
     orientation and searing
               (MORE)

Out   of   frustration,   Susan   slaps   the
Professor.

          PROFESSOR WHEN (CONT'D)
     Arhh!
     I do wish that you would desist with
     this repetitive physical assault upon
     my person.

                    SUSAN
     Call it a toaster.

               PROFESSOR WHEN
     Toaster is simply the acronym. It is
     in fact a time orientation and

Susan slaps him again.

               PROFESSOR WHEN
     Arhh!

                    SUSAN
     Call it a toaster.

               PROFESSOR WHEN
     I will not be bullied in this manner.

                    TRENT
     Susan. Professor. Sinking ship!
     Let's go home, while we can.

The Professor giggles at Trent's naive
comment.

                PROFESSOR WHEN
     Oh, my boy. The ship will take hours
     to sink. We don't have to panic.

                    TRENT
     I just think that we should go now.
     Before anything else goes wrong.

                PROFESSOR WHEN
                  (giggling.)
     Oh, what could possibly go wrong?

There is a huge explosion nearby. As the
Professor is propelled, he makes a grab for
the toaster.

EXT. BESIDE THE TITANIC, IN THE OCEAN. AFTER MIDNIGHT

The Professor, Susan and Trent find themselves coughing and spluttering in the very cold North Atlantic Ocean.

The Professor is clutching the toaster and desperately trying to keep it out of the water.

There is a great deal of panic.

> TRENT
> Oh, no!
> I don't want to drown in the
> North Atlantic.
> ...And I don't need another bath!

> SUSAN
> It's very cold in the North Atlantic,
> Professor. What now?

> PROFESSOR WHEN
> Swim to me!
> I have the Time ...thingy.

Trent sees the Professor's difficulty in keeping the toaster above water.

> TRENT
> Is the toaster designed to float
> in water, Professor?

                    PROFESSOR WHEN
Don't be ridiculous!
Why would I invent an amphibious
toaster? Whoever heard of such a
thing? ...But now that you mention the
concept.

                       SUSAN
Swim while he's prattling, Trent.
It saves time.

Susan and Trent swim to the Professor.

                    PROFESSOR WHEN
Good! Now everybody hold hands and I
will touch the eating utensil that is

Susan touches the knife.

INT. INSIDE THE TOASTER. ARTIFICIAL LIGHTING

All is not well. Water is flowing into the toaster.

> PROFESSOR WHEN
> I said that I would touch the

> SUSAN
> I would have drowned before you finished talking about it.

> TRENT
> Professor, there's water coming in. The toaster is sinking!

> PROFESSOR WHEN
> Well, let's get out of here. If the circuitry gets wet, it won't work.

The Professor stops mid-panic and gives Trent a serious, questioning look.

> PROFESSOR WHEN
> Please tell me that you still have the capacitor.

> TRENT
> I still have the capacitor, Professor. Here it is.

Trent hands the capacitor to the Professor who opens a compartment on the console and begins replacing the old capacitor.

The Professor stops his work to talk to
Trent.

>   PROFESSOR WHEN
>   Good boy! I'm really quite impressed.
>   With a bit of training, you and I
>   could be quite a team.

>   SUSAN
>   (sarcasm.)
>   I had noticed this.

>   TRENT
>   Thank you, Professor.

>   SUSAN
>   Could you both stop talking long
>   enough to fix the toaster?

>   PROFESSOR WHEN
>   Young lady, you could learn a
>   great deal from this young man
>   about staying cool in a situation.

>   SUSAN
>   He's not cool.
>   He's just dead from the neck up.

The Professor shakes his head and returns to
the console. He presses the capacitor into
place and closes the compartment.

>   PROFESSOR WHEN
>   There! It's fixed.

The water flow suddenly increases. In panic,
Trent states the obvious.

> TRENT
> Professor, the water is pouring in.
> The circuitry is getting wet.

The Professor panics.

> PROFESSOR WHEN
> Press a button, lad.

Trent panics.

> TRENT
> Which one?

> SUSAN
> Now he gets particular.
> Any one, Dumbo. Get us out of here.

> TRENT
> OK. The orange one.

> PROFESSOR WHEN
> No!
> Not the orange button marked
> Space Travel.

There is an electrical explosion and clunking mechanical noises. The lights flash off and on.

The scene goes to black but we hear Professor When's empty voice screaming through time and space.

> PROFESSOR WHEN (V.O.)
> Oh buggarrrrr!

INT. INSIDE THE TOASTER. ARTIFICIAL LIGHTING

The toaster has arrived at its destination. The lights are on. The Professor is sitting despondently in a puddle on the floor. Susan and Trent look on in silence.

TRENT
Can we help, Professor?

PROFESSOR WHEN
(sarcasm.)
No. I think you've both done quite enough for one day. Thank you.

Trent tries some humour.

TRENT
Yeah, but which day was it?
The day at Troy or the day we landed on the Titanic or this day now?

The Professor only looks up with a black look before returning to his sulk.

SUSAN
Oh, come on. Cheer up.
We're no worse off.

There is no response. Susan searches for a positive.

SUSAN
The toaster is fixed.
Capacitor replaced!
Most of the water has drained away.

Still no response.

> SUSAN
> We just need to find some intelligent
> life form to tell us what the date and
> time is and

> PROFESSOR WHEN
> We are no longer on the planet, Earth.

There is a moment of stunned silence while
Susan absorbs his words.

> SUSAN
> So, ...maybe we are just a little
> bit worse off.

The Professor takes a deep breath and drags
himself up. He turns on a monitor on the
console.

> TRENT
> So, where are we, Professor?

> PROFESSOR WHEN
> The only thing that I can ascertain
> with any degree of certainty is that
> we have not left our Universe.

> SUSAN
> (sarcasm.)
> Oh, wonderful.

> TRENT
> How do you know that, Professor?

                    PROFESSOR WHEN
Because the I.U.T. button is the
only button that you haven't
pressed, during your brief time
near this console.

                    SUSAN
What does I.U.T. stand for,
Professor?

                    TRENT
Is it even possible to leave
our Universe?

                    PROFESSOR WHEN
Yes, it certainly is but you should
wish that it never happens. You cannot
conceive of the consequences
...the boggling of the mind!

                    SUSAN
Oh, yes, we can conceive of the
boggling.
We have seen it in action.
What does I.U.T. stand for, Professor?

                    PROFESSOR WHEN
I.U.T. stands for Inter Universe
Travel.

                    TRENT
I.U.T. isn't much of an acronym.
Iut doesn't really mean anything,
does it?

The Professor is frustrated with the course of this conversation.

           PROFESSOR WHEN
    It is not an acronym. It is an
    abbreviation!

               SUSAN
    Why didn't you make an acronym
    for it?

               TRENT
    Yeah. You usually do acronyms.
    I didn't know what an acronym was
    until I met you and now I can use
    it in a sentence.

           PROFESSOR WHEN
    It's just a button! It's not a
    multi-purpose tool! You just press
    it to make something happen.

               TRENT
    Why didn't you just call it
    'Inter Universe Travel'?

           PROFESSOR WHEN
      (even more frustrated.)
    Because it didn't fit on the button!
    I would have needed a bigger button!

               SUSAN
    OK! Cool down everyone.
    What say we go outside?

           PROFESSOR WHEN
    Oh, yes please!

```
                    TRENT
    Yep.

Susan grabs them both and leans against the
really big knife.
```

Trent & Susan.
The perfect T.O.A.S.T.E.R. Crew.

Photography by Noel Clarke (Noelyn Studios).

INT. INSIDE A GREY METAL CORRIDOR.
ARTIFICIAL LIGHTING

The three stare around but there are only
metal walls, a metal floor and a metal
ceiling. There is no clue to indicate where
they are. Trent tucks the toaster under his
arm.

                    TRENT
        Where are we, Professor?

The Professor stares at Trent, trying to
determine his actual level of 'dumb'.

                  PROFESSOR WHEN
              (sarcasm.)
          Oh, look! We appear to be in a
          long, metal corridor, somewhere
          in our Universe.

Trent and the Professor stare at each other,
both obstinately out staring the other.
After an awkward silence, Susan intercedes.

                    SUSAN
          Let's go for a walk, boys, and see
          if we can find an intelligent life
          form to talk to about going home.

                  PROFESSOR WHEN
        Good plan.

They walk down the corridor.

INT. INSIDE A WHITE METAL CORRIDOR.
ARTIFICIAL LIGHTING

A RED ALIEN slithers along the metal floor
leaving behind a slime trail. As it
struggles to move along the floor, the
voices of the Professor, Susan and Trent can
be heard in the distance.

> PROFESSOR WHEN (V.O.)
> I suggest we go this way.

> SUSAN (V.O.)
> We've already been that way.

> TRENT (V.O.)
> I'm confused. All these corridors
> look the same.

> SUSAN (V.O.)
> Look! That one is painted white.
> We haven't been in a white corridor
> before.

> PROFESSOR WHEN (V.O.)
> We should navigate our way down
> the white corridor, then.

The alien listens and then slithers to the
wall and opens a panel, revealing a number
of buttons. With great difficulty, he
presses one with his slimy, jelly-like
finger.

There is a noise of dozens of tiny wheels running on a metal floor, with a background purr of little motors.

Cut to a close up of the tiny wheels at the base of small TIN CANS that are whizzing over the metal floor of a corridor. We don't see the top of the tin cans.

Cut back to the alien who is still lying next to his panel, listening intently to the approaching noise of the tin cans and, from the other direction, the growing volume of the voices.

> SUSAN (V.O.)
> Can anyone else hear a noise?

> TRENT (V.O.)
> It sounds like remote control cars.

> PROFESSOR WHEN (V.O.)
> My dear boy, why would there be remote control cars?

> TRENT (V.O.)
> I said 'sounds like'.

> SUSAN (V.O.)
> Please stop talking.

The alien slithers to another panel and opens it to reveal a large, extra-terrestrial rifle. As the alien pulls it out of the panel, water flows out of the rifle onto the floor. The alien shakes its head in frustration.

RED ALIEN
Gnarrs non nimper poten!

The alien presses buttons on the rifle and
shakes it. Slowly the red light faintly
glows and then goes out. It is dead.

RED ALIEN
Gnarrs non nimper poten!

The sound of approaching tin cans has been
growing louder. The noise of the wheels
stops, leaving just the purring of many
motors. The alien knows that they have
arrived and his face contorts into what is
probably a sinister smile.

INT. INSIDE THE SAME WHITE METAL CORRIDOR.
ARTIFICIAL LIGHTING

The Professor, Susan and Trent round a bend
in the corridor and find themselves
confronting a slimy, red alien, lying
prostrate on the floor, with a small band of
wheeled tin cans purring behind it.

Susan and Trent are repulsed at the sight of
the alien and worried about their first
encounter with an alien life form. The
Professor is immediately excited.

                    PROFESSOR WHEN
          My dear friend, Torgish!

The red alien eyes his dead rifle with
disgust.

                    RED ALIEN
          Gnarrs non nimper poten!

The Professor dives into the pockets of his
coat and finds the B.E.L.T. He points it
toward the alien.

The alien cowers as the B.E.L.T. is aimed at
him.

                    PROFESSOR WHEN
          Please forgive me, my dear, long
          lost friend. I wasn't expecting
          company and didn't have my
          Language Translator ready.
          What were you saying, Torgish?

                      RED ALIEN
          We didn't mean it. I'm sorry!

                       TRENT
          Is that thing friendly, Professor?

The alien eyes them all suspiciously.

The   Professor   is   shocked   at   Trent's
insulting words.

                    PROFESSOR WHEN
          Manners, my boy!
          This is my great friend, Torgish!

Torgish   gives   the   rifle   a   subtle   hit.
Nothing happens. He casts the Professor an
attempt at a friendly 'smile'.

                      RED ALIEN
          So, Professor. You have survived
          to visit my planet, yet again.

                       SUSAN
          You've been here before, Professor?

                    PROFESSOR WHEN
          Yes. A long time ago ...I think.
          It's hard to tell without a
          time reference.

                         TRENT
          What does he mean by 'survived',
          Professor?

The Professor shakes his head and taps the
B.E.L.T. against the palm of his hand.

                    PROFESSOR WHEN
          It is a language translation thing.
          For some reason, the B.E.L.T. has
          never worked well on Torgish's
          language. It approximates the meaning.
          Very confusing sometimes.

The Professor points the B.E.L.T. more
intently at the alien as if it would improve
its operation. The alien cowers again.

                    PROFESSOR WHEN
          How long has it been since my last
          visit, Torgish?

The alien's eyes narrow and it hisses its
reply.

                       RED ALIEN
          We haven't been cursed with your
          presence for over thirty of our years.

Trent and Susan are both very wary of the
alien's unfriendly demeanour.

> SUSAN
> Professor! 'Cursed'?
> I don't think it likes you.

> PROFESSOR WHEN
> Oh, nonsense! Torgish and I go back
> a long way. It was he who first sent
> for me to consult on improvements to
> his planets power systems.

> TRENT
> But it said 'cursed with your
> presence', Professor. Surely, you
> can see that it doesn't like you?

> PROFESSOR WHEN
> Nonsense! I told you it's an L.T.
> thing. The language translator often
> gives me antonyms of the real meaning.

> SUSAN / TRENT
> What?

The Professor addresses the alien.

> PROFESSOR WHEN
> Pardon me, Torgish. These young
> people today! So much to learn
> about travel and technology.

The Professor smiles broadly at his old
friend before addressing Susan and Trent.

The red alien gives the rifle another shake.
The red light dimly glows before failing
again. The alien mumbles to itself.

>   PROFESSOR WHEN
> 'Antonym' is the word that means
> the opposite to the word you have.
> For example 'bad' is the antonym
> of 'good'.
> Torgish said 'cursed' so he meant...

The Professor leaves the sentence hanging so
that Susan or Trent can provide the correct
answer. They both stare at him in silence,
waiting for him to finish the sentence. The
Professor's eyes narrow as he stares into
the blank faces. He moves to end the failed
lesson.

>   PROFESSOR WHEN
> Torgish said 'cursed' so he meant
> 'blessed', obviously.
> Now, back to talking to my friend.

>   TRENT
> I don't think that is what he meant.

>   SUSAN
> He doesn't like you. You can read it
> in the body language and facial
> expressions.

>   PROFESSOR WHEN
> Rubbish! You can't read a blob
> of jelly.

The Professor turns to Torgish and realises what he has said. He giggles with embarrassment at his remark.

> PROFESSOR WHEN
> Oh, please excuse me, my old friend.
> That was just a little insensitive.

The alien spits out his words in anger.

> RED ALIEN
> I once stood upright like you.
> My body was once similar to your
> body. We walked on two, solid legs.
> Our skin pigment was like yours.
> My people once passed unnoticed on
> your planet.

> TRENT
> Wow! What went wrong?

The Professor hastens to change the subject.

> PROFESSOR WHEN
> Oh, we don't need to go into that.
> It is a very long, boring story.
> How are my good friends, Manish,
> Deshan and ...Tim?

> RED ALIEN
> Apparently, very dead
> ...as you would know.

The Professor looks with frustration at the B.E.L.T. and gives it a vigorous shake.

                    PROFESSOR WHEN
        I'm very pleased to hear that their
        condition is good. Please give them
        my regards.

The alien shrinks back with fear and grips
his dead rifle.

                    TRENT
        This L.T. thing is really weird,
        Professor. Who are Manish, Deshan
        and Tim?

                    SUSAN
        It's not a language translation,
        antonym thing. Listen to his words.

She is ignored by both Trent and the
Professor.

                    PROFESSOR WHEN
        Manish, Deshan, Tim and Torgish run
        this planet as a council. All brothers
        who look very much alike except for
        their colours. Manish is orange, Deshan
        is green and Tim is yellow.

                    SUSAN
        That's a big job for four ...um
        people. What is the planet's
        population?

PROFESSOR WHEN
Oh, yes, there were billions the last
time I was here. Torgish, what is the
current population of your planet?

RED ALIEN
I suppose you would like me to count
myself and my brothers in the
calculation?

PROFESSOR WHEN
Yes, of course. Always keen to get
the accurate picture. No point in
statistics unless there is some
precision.

RED ALIEN
Four.

Stunned silence falls on the room.

PROFESSOR WHEN
Four?
Four billion?

RED ALIEN
Four. Without the billion.
Just 'four'.

The Professor is embarrassed. Susan and
Trent are amazed.

PROFESSOR WHEN
Four? Well, that is a substantial
decline. No overcrowding in the
subway here.

RED ALIEN
We needed the extra nuclear power
from the project that we employed
you for. We had used up this planet.
We wanted to invade, and slaughter,
the inhabitants of the third planet
in the Delta Solar System.

SUSAN
Professor?

TRENT
Wow! You've been naughty, Professor.

PROFESSOR WHEN
To be fair, they didn't tell me
that at the time. I was keen to help
because they told me they needed
extra power to make life better for
the population.
It wasn't until later that I found
out the truth.
And the whole population knew the
truth and everybody lied to me!

RED ALIEN
And you failed us!

PROFESSOR WHEN
No! My designs were excellent.
Not just the nuclear ones ...but all
of the things I designed and built
while I was here.
I made you that rifle!

The alien shakes the rifle and it springs
into life with a green light. Its eyes widen
in excitement but the rifle immediately dies
again. It curses in frustration.

RED ALIEN
Built by Professor When!

PROFESSOR WHEN
The problem was the solar wind from
that Super Nova.

TRENT
You've got to watch that solar wind.

SUSAN
Stay with us, Trent.

TRENT
Sorry.

RED ALIEN
The Super Nova would not have made
us glow in the dark and melt to slimy
jelly and change colour.

PROFESSOR WHEN
Could have.

                    SUSAN
I've heard they can do that.

                    TRENT
Yep.

                  RED ALIEN
And quadrupled our gravity so that
our bodies are squashed to the ground
so badly that we have to live
underground in this artificial
environment.

                    TRENT
Oh, that's definitely a Nova
Super thingy.

                    SUSAN
One of the main effects, I've heard.

The Professor gives Susan and Trent an
acknowledging nod for their support.

                 PROFESSOR WHEN
I really don't think you can blame
any of this on me, Torgish.
I applied my superior intellect
to solve your problem and a freak
of nature intervened.

                    TRENT
Is he talking about me?

                    SUSAN
Not this time. A different freak
of nature.

The alien shakes the rifle. It is still
dead.

>   RED ALIEN
>   Enough of this.
>   I will have my revenge.

>   PROFESSOR WHEN
>   Young lady, you were quite
>   accurate, by the way.

>   SUSAN
>   What?

>   RED ALIEN
>   K.A.I.T., activate.

>   PROFESSOR WHEN
>   The L.T. is working perfectly.
>   He really doesn't like me.

The sound of purring motors, behind the
alien, intensifies.

>   SUSAN
>   No, he doesn't, Professor.

>   PROFESSOR WHEN
>   I really think we should move
>   along the corridor in a direction
>   that takes us away, with speed,
>   from these tin cans, that would
>   appear to be dangerous to our health.

>   TRENT
>   (to Susan.)
>   What'd he say?

                    SUSAN
    He said 'Run'!

The Professor, Susan and Trent turn to run
away just as another group of tin cans
appear around the corner. The alien sputters
a horrible, evil laugh.

                  RED ALIEN
    You cannot escape, Professor.
    You are surrounded.

The Professor, Susan and Trent await their
fate.

                  RED ALIEN
    K.A.I.T., prepare to fire.

                PROFESSOR WHEN
    I really think we should talk
    about this, Torgish. After all,
    we have been friends for a long time.

The inhabitants of the tin cans show their
heads as they prepare to fire. They are the
fluffiest, cutest kittens with big adorable
eyes.

                    SUSAN
    O.M.G! They are so cute.

                    TRENT
    Ooh! I was so scared, I almost wet
    my pants. Look at those adorable
    kittens.

                    PROFESSOR WHEN
Oh, Torgish. You really had us
going for a minute there,
my old friend.

The alien looks perplexed at their reaction.

                    TRENT
Why are the cute kittens in tins,
Professor?

                    PROFESSOR WHEN
Because they are kaits, my boy.

                    SUSAN
Yes. We know what they are,
Professor, but Trent asked why they
are in tins? And the pronunciation
is 'cats'.

                    PROFESSOR WHEN
No. The earthly resemblance is to
cats but

                    RED ALIEN
Can we get on with this?

                    PROFESSOR WHEN
Shush, Torgish. Education of young
people in progress.

                    RED ALIEN
Education is a waste of time if
          (MORE)

PROFESSOR WHEN
I had forgotten about these life
forms. You observe so many different
variations on life that you cannot
be expected to remember.

RED ALIEN (CONT'D)
...grotesque death is imminent.

PROFESSOR WHEN
You see K.A.I.T. is an acronym for
Cute Alien In Tin.

TRENT
Aww ...that's a nice acronym.
They're gorgeous!

SUSAN
So, that makes the acronym 'C.A.I.T.',
doesn't it?

RED ALIEN
Would like to get on with my plan.

PROFESSOR WHEN
No, no, no ...no!
The acronym is 'K.A.I.T.'.

TRENT
It really doesn't matter, people.
It's just nice that they're cute and
not the killers we thought they were.

> SUSAN
Of course it matters!
'Cute' does not start with a 'K'.

The red alien has become very impatient. He points to one of the kaits.

> RED ALIEN
You! Warning shot over their heads.

The kait looks up and laser rays fire from its eyes. The ceiling explodes and rubble falls down onto everyone.

> PROFESSOR WHEN
Killer! Killer starts with K.
The acronym is 'K.A.I.T.'.
Killer Alien In Tin.

Susan and Trent look, wide eyed, at each other.

> TRENT
Well, I'm glad we sorted that out.

> SUSAN
Can we leave now, Professor?

> RED ALIEN
No-one leaves. There will be some dying.

The Professor studies the situation and walks over to the alien. The alien cowers as the Professor leans over him.

                    PROFESSOR WHEN
A point of negotiation, Torgish.

                      RED ALIEN
I have kaits.
I don't need to negotiate.
          (MORE)

As it talks, the rifle in the alien's hands
fires up and the light turns green. It grins
broadly (I think) and looks at the Professor
with excited eyes.

                 RED ALIEN (CONT'D)
And I have the rifle that you built.
          (MORE)

At the completion of the sentence, the rifle
dies. The alien is deflated.

                 RED ALIEN (CONT'D)
I have kaits!

                    PROFESSOR WHEN
Yes, Torgish, you have kaits. But
I saw the excitement in your eyes
when you thought you may be able to
kill me with my own weapon.
That would be the perfect result
wouldn't it?

                    RED ALIEN
That would be the way of my people.
That would be my perfect revenge.
But I will settle for using the kaits.

                 PROFESSOR WHEN
But what if you don't have to settle,
Torgish?

                    RED ALIEN
I'm listening.

                 PROFESSOR WHEN
Good. It should never have got to
this point. You should have just
called me and told me that you
were unhappy with the results of
my project.

                    RED ALIEN
I mean I'm listening to the
alternate way of killing you.

                 PROFESSOR WHEN
Oh, yes. Sorry. Misunderstood!

The Professor puts his hand into his coat
and pulls out the C.A.P.S.U.L.E.

                 PROFESSOR WHEN
This, too, is a weapon that I
designed and built.

                     SUSAN
Professor, what are you doing?

                    TRENT
Don't give him the capsule.

                  RED ALIEN
It's a toy gun with a suction cup.

The Professor smiles knowingly at the alien.

                PROFESSOR WHEN
You're not the first to make that
erroneous judgement.

                  RED ALIEN
What are you proposing?
Given that it might be a weapon.

                    TRENT
Oh, it's a weapon all right.

                    SUSAN
One shot! Hundreds died!
I saw it with my own eyes.

The Professor casts Susan a dirty look.

                PROFESSOR WHEN
They were going to die anyway.

                  RED ALIEN
What are you proposing?

                PROFESSOR WHEN
Let my young friends go free and I
will allow you to shoot me with it.

                    SUSAN
Aww, Professor!

                    TRENT
That's really nice of you,
Professor. I'm gunna miss you
when you're dead.

The Professor's train of thought is
interrupted while he considers Trent's
comment. He gives him a black look.

                PROFESSOR WHEN
After all, they weren't involved in
the Super Nova, were they?

                  RED ALIEN
The Super Nova had nothing to do
with it.

                PROFESSOR WHEN
Either way, they weren't involved,
were they?

                  RED ALIEN
No. I suppose they can go.
How does this capsule work?

                PROFESSOR WHEN
You just press this purple button
and then count to twelve and it
will be fully charged.

The alien moves to press the purple button.

                PROFESSOR WHEN
Hold on!

                    RED ALIEN
What now?

                  PROFESSOR WHEN
I just need to take my young friends
to the end of the corridor and explain
to them how they can get home.
Is that acceptable to you?

                    RED ALIEN
Yes, but be reminded, Professor,
that you cannot outrun my kaits.

                  PROFESSOR WHEN
Oh, I don't intend running.
I have given you my word.
You may now press the purple button.

                    RED ALIEN
You have been a worthy adversary,
Professor. You have outwitted and
terminated my dumb, assassin brothers.

The Professor looks with all the compassion
he can muster.

                  PROFESSOR WHEN
Yes. Well. Not much of a compliment
when you really think about it.

The remark doesn't appear to register. The
alien depresses the purple button.

                    RED ALIEN
One, Two,

                    PROFESSOR WHEN
Come, Susan. Trent.
To the end of the corridor.
I will explain how to go home.

                         TRENT
This is really nice of you,
Professor. Dying for us like this.

                    PROFESSOR WHEN
I have no intention of dying,
my boy.

                         TRENT
But you gave him your capsule.
He pressed the purple button.

                        SUSAN
Do you have a plan, Professor?

They continue walking toward the bend in the
corridor. The Professor is indignant that
the question has even been asked.

                    PROFESSOR WHEN
Of course I have a plan.

                       RED ALIEN
Eight, nine

                    PROFESSOR WHEN
Quickly, around the corner.

There is a huge explosion. Tins bounce off
the walls and ceiling. A red splatter of
slimy jelly covers the walls of the
previously white corridor.

PROFESSOR WHEN
Quickly, into the time orientation

There is an electrical explosion.

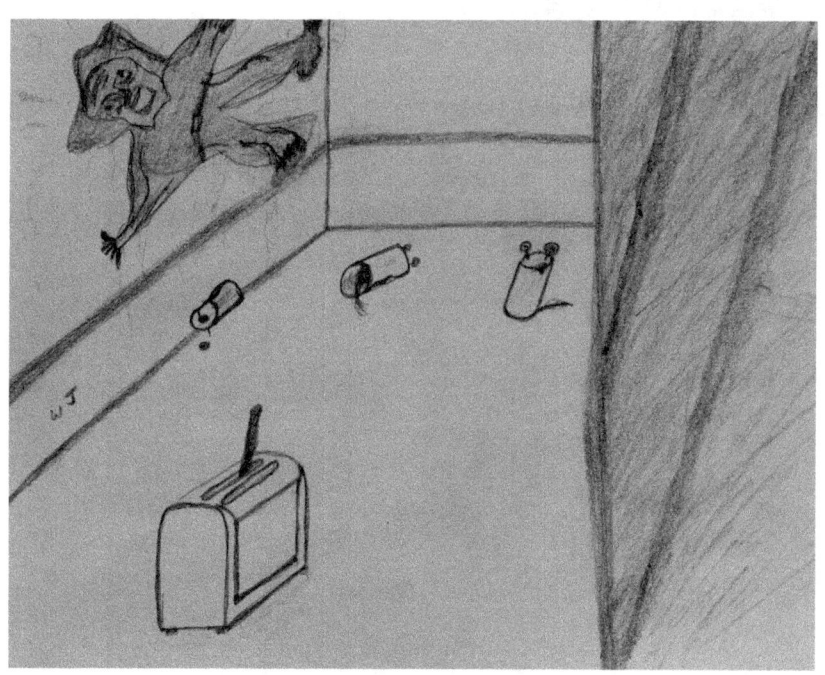

INT. INSIDE THE TOASTER. ARTIFICIAL LIGHTING

The Professor goes immediately to the console and begins adjusting the settings.

> TRENT
> Professor, you fibbed.
> You didn't let him shoot you.

> PROFESSOR WHEN
> It wasn't a gun, my boy.

> SUSAN
> So the dual purpose of the capsule was as a bomb?

The Professor is still busy calibrating his instruments.

> PROFESSOR WHEN
> Capsule stands for 'Can Actually Propel Stuff Utilising Liquid Explosive'.
> The button had a ten second delay.

> TRENT
> Ooh! You told him to count to twelve.
> Fibber!

> SUSAN
> Why would you think you would ever need a bomb?

PROFESSOR WHEN
It wasn't a bomb. It was a propellant.
In case I ever needed to propel
...stuff.

SUSAN
Professor. This is bigger than the
Titanic. You just killed the last
person ...thingy ...on this planet.

PROFESSOR WHEN
The Super Nova got the other three
billion. Anyway, they were all
psychopaths. They destroyed their
own planet.

SUSAN
Super Nova?

TRENT
What did they do that was so bad?

PROFESSOR WHEN
Think about it! There aren't all
that many inhabitable planets.
Where do you think the third planet
in the Delta Solar System might be?
You remember! The planet they were
going to invade and kill all of the
inhabitants.

The Professor is still calibrating his
instruments.

                    SUSAN
Not good at astronomical games.

                    TRENT
Nope. Don't know.

               PROFESSOR WHEN
Third planet is a hint.

                    SUSAN
Ooh.

                    TRENT
Nope. Still don't know.

Susan whispers in Trent's ear.

                    TRENT
Ooh.

                    SUSAN
You're spending a lot of time on
this setting, Professor.

                    TRENT
Yeah. You just did a quick twiddle
last time.

               PROFESSOR WHEN
Torgish told me how long it had
been since I was last here and I
know what planet we're on.
I can take us straight home.

The toaster is rocked by an explosion,
throwing the Professor and Susan to the
floor. Trent hangs onto the console.

PROFESSOR WHEN
We need to get out of here
quickly. The kaits are attacking
our time orient

As he talks, the Professor struggles to his
feet but another explosion rocks the toaster
and sends him back to the floor.

TRENT
It's alright, Professor.
I've got this.

PROFESSOR WHEN
No, my boy. It's set to
(MORE)

Trent makes a lunge at the button when
another explosion rocks the toaster. He
smacks the wrong button.

There is an electrical explosion and
clunking, mechanical noises. The lighting
turns red and sirens sound through the
depths of the toaster.

PROFESSOR WHEN (CONT'D)
Oh no! You've hit the I.U.T. button.

Lights flash. Explosions occur throughout
the toaster. Sirens grow louder. Bedlam.

SUSAN
I don't want to go to another
Universe!

                    TRENT
      I'm still confused by this one.

A final explosion. Everything goes black.
Silence.

                  SUSAN (V.O.)
      Oh, buggar!

                  THE END.

Between recording:
Trent Wilson, Wayne Jarman, Michael Ford, Susan McEwen,
Gareth Jarman, Shayne Bartlett & Lindi Jarman.

Photography by Noel Clarke (Noelyn Studios).